UNHOLY

Unholy

By Erin Trejo

Cover Design: Shepard Originals with Amanda Shepard

Copyright 2024@Erintrejo

No part of this publication may be reproduced or transmitted in any form or by any means, electronic or mechanical, including photocopy, recording, or any information storage and retrieval system without the prior written consent from the author, except in the instance of quotes for reviews. No part of this book may be scanned, uploaded, or distributed via the Internet without the permission of the author, which is a violation of the International copyright law and subjects the violator to severe fines and imprisonment.

This is a work of fiction. The names, characters, incidents and places are products of the author's imagination, and are not to be construed as real except where noted and authorized. Any resemblance to persons, living or dead, or actual events are entirely coincidental. Any trademarks, service marks, product names, names featured are assumed to be the property of their respective owners, and are used only for reference. There is no implied endorsement if any of these terms are used.

Note from the author:

"Welcome to the dark side where nothing is off limits. You want to be spanked and called a good girl? You want to kneel at my altar of all that is me? Drop to your knees pretty girl and show me what that mouth can do."

-Tristan

Chapter 1
Tristan

I kick my feet up on the table in front of me, crossing my ankles as I glare at the doctor. Then I reach over and grab a doughnut off the plate and pull a piece off, popping it into my mouth.

"So, what is it today, Doc?" I ask him. "Still a psychopath?" I ask him while I chew. I pull another piece off and shove it in my mouth while I wait for the asshole to answer. I only come here because my mom asks me too. Well, that and a little legal trouble.

"Tristan, you've been coming here since you were three. I still don't know how to categorize you. You're not typical of anything," he tells me like this is the first time. It isn't. I just like to hear him say it.

"Then why am I still here?" I ask him, shoving the rest of the food into my mouth.

"Court order says you're to be here," he reminds me. I smirk.

"Court orders. Who gives a fuck what the court orders? They don't know me. They don't know shit about me."

"They know enough to know you need to be here."

"Do you think I need to be here?" I ask him in a condescending tone.

"As I said, you've been coming here since you were three. So, in that case, yes, I do."

"We go over the same shit every time I'm here. Nothing changes aside from my meds if I decide to take them."

"And you should be taking them, Tristan. They'll help, but you don't give them time to do that," he tells me.

"Have you taken them?" he shakes his head.

"No."

"Then you have no idea how the hell they make you feel. One second, you want to claw your fucking skin off, and the next, you're too lost in a fog to even know you have skin," I tell him.

"We can change them if they give you side effects," he suggests as if I haven't heard this before.

"Doc, I hate meds, okay? I hate how they make me feel. I hate how it makes everything around me dull. Frankly, I just hate them."

"Then you have no choice but to keep coming here until you are med-compliant, Tristan."

"Then I suppose you're going to see more and fucking more of me, aren't you, Doc?" His face never changes. Not a single bit.

He's always got this bored, hard as fuck exterior I can't seem to get around. Most others, I can, but not him. Doctor Hassan has been treating me since I was three.

Three fucking years old, and I was coming to this prick just because my mom didn't know how to handle me.

I was a bad kid who grew into a bad teenager and then grew into a bad adult. What fucking more did she need to know?

But I love my mom. At least as much as someone like me can love. The good old Doc here says I use her to get what I want, and maybe he's right. Maybe that's exactly what I do to her. Maybe he's wrong? Who the hell am I to say?

I check the time and see I've been here for the hour I'm supposed to be here. I let my feet drop back onto the floor before standing and saluting the asshole.

"Until next week, Doc." I head for the door when he speaks, stopping me.

"You know she's worried about you with the upcoming wedding." I cringe not needing to be reminded of that shit.

"Well, she has no reason to worry. I'll be on my best little behavior," I tell him.

"I mean it, Tristan. She thinks this marriage is going to be what pushes you over the edge." Now, I snort a laugh.

"Sorry, Doc. Times up," I remind him before pulling the door open and walking out of his office.

I head through the waiting area and out the main door to where my mom is waiting.

"How'd it go?"

"Same as always," I reply.

"Did he give you new meds?" I nod my head, lying to her.

"Yeah. I'll give them a try," I lie to her again. He didn't give me shit, and I sure as hell aren't going to try anything new either. I wish she would understand this, but she doesn't.

"Good. Did you talk about the wedding?" she asks softly. I rest my hand on her shoulder and nod.

"I'm fine, Mom. As long as he treats you well, that's all I'm concerned about."

"You know he does, Tristan."

"Then I'm happy for you. Let's go. I'm starving." She smiles and we both climb in the car before she takes off.

"I did tell you that Ash is moving in with us too, right?"

"Yeah. I'm thinking about moving into the warehouse anyway. It's almost ready." I have a warehouse. My dad left it to me when he died a long ass time ago, and I converted it into a livable space. That's where I spend a lot of my time.

"You don't have to do that. I think it'll be nice having us all under one roof, at least for a little while. Will you at least think about it?" she asks, pulling into the restaurant parking lot.

"Yeah, of course. Maybe just a few months until I finish upgrading the warehouse," I tell her, just to make her happy. I highly doubt I'm going to stay at my mom's any longer than I already have, considering I'm twenty-five fucking years old.

"Good. Let's go eat. Ash will be here tonight, so you'll finally get to meet her," she says excitedly. I'm not as thrilled as she is, but for her I can do this.

We climb out of the car and head inside, where she leads me over to the table.

"Ted." She bends down, pressing a kiss to his cheek. He doesn't even greet her like a normal person should, and that makes me sick to my fucking stomach and ready to gut the bastard with my knife.

"Amy. Tristan."

"What's up, Ted?"

"This is Ash," he announces, motioning across the table to his daughter. My eyes move to meet hers, and that's where I'm lost. Big brown eyes gaze back at me with a mix of fear and intrigue.

Not that I would give her the time of day aside from playing with her a little. She's a fucking bible thumper, just like her dad. And my mom, apparently.

"Take a seat," Ted says, causing me to pull my gaze away from his precious little daughter. I drop down into the seat next to her, sliding a little closer than I need to. Ted orders for everyone, annoying me further as conversation picks up between him and my mom. I turn to Ash and start to stare at her, making her uncomfortable.

"I'll be-" I don't let her finish her sentence. I lower my hand under the table and rest it on her thigh. Her breath instantly hitches as she slowly turns her head to look at me.

"What are you doing?" she whispers.

"What do you mean? I'm getting to know my new sister."

"Move your hand," she hisses at me.

"Nah, I like it there."

"I'll tell."

"Oh no. Not a tattletale. What will I do?" I ask her in a condescending tone.

"Move your hand," she demands, and I squeeze her leg a little tighter. She moves her hand under the table, trying to pry my hand off her, but it does no good. I'm not moving it until I'm damn good and ready.

"What is wrong with you?"

"Me? You're the one being a little bitch," I tell her. Her mouth parts, her cheeks turn pink, and I realize she has never been called that before. I smirk, knowing I'm the first.

"So, Tristan. Your mom tells me you've been doing some work recently."

"I have."

"What are you working on?" he asks as if he's really interested in me. He isn't. He knows I'm a fuck up, just like everyone else does. He only pretends to care because of my mom.

"Sculptures, mostly. Some rich prick saw my work and wanted his own," I answer as I grab the glass of water in front of me and bring it to my lips.

"What kind of sculptures?"

"The kind that would have your little nun here clutching her pearls," I tell him. My mom chokes on her water and quickly sets it back on the table while I take my down, finishing the glass.

"So something interesting then."

"Nude women. He likes the sculptures of nude women. In fact, he's so well off he even sends me a nude model to work off," I add. I can feel Ash tense under my grip and it makes me smile knowing she's that uncomfortable.

"Really? Well, that is something else," he says before our food arrives. Now that I have to eat, I pull my hand away from Ash and grab my knife and fork.

"Tristan is really good at what he does. That piece near the courthouse, the horse? That's his work," my mom chimes in, trying to make me sound like a better person than I am. I shake my head, not wanting her to say a word, but that gets Ted all interested again.

7

"Really? That is quite a piece of work. Do you make it all by hand?" he asks, and I nod.

"I like to work with my hands," I reply, glancing at Ash out of the corner of my eye. She knows I'm looking at her she's just too shy to admit it.

The rest of dinner goes by in a blur of them talking about religious shit that I have no interest in, so I zone out.

Chapter 2
Ash

"What do you mean he grabbed you?" Ben, my boyfriend, asks me. I didn't want to tell him, but it felt wrong not to.

"He grabbed my leg under the table."

"Did you tell your dad?" I shake my head as I play with the straw in my milkshake.

"No. It didn't seem appropriate to bring it up at dinner. His mom was there. I think he was just trying to get to me."

"I don't like the idea of him being under the same roof as you. I think I should talk with your dad about this," Ben says, but I shake my head.

"I don't want to make things worse. I have a lot going on anyway with studying and everything. I doubt I'll ever see him. Dad said he was setting up a room for him in the basement anyway," I add.

"That's probably where he belongs." Ben mumbles.

"Don't be like that. He's just … different, is all."

"He isn't religious. I'm surprised your dad is even letting him in the house. He probably worships the devil in his free time." I laugh a little, but I wouldn't doubt that one bit. Not judging him on looks alone. Not that he's an ugly man because he is far from it. He's very good-looking with shaggy dark hair and a smile I'm sure could melt a girl's insides.

"Oh, don't worry. Dad will get to him, I'm sure. He always does."

"Not if he's as bad as you say he is."

"I don't know how bad he is, Ben. I just know what I observed," I remind him.

Ben has been my boyfriend for the last three years. Dad approved of him because he goes to the same church as we do. He's met his parents, and they are both very Godly people. Ben is smart and sweet and everything a girl could ask for.

"You want to go for a walk?" Ben asks as we sit on the front porch. I nod my head, and he offers his hand, helping me up.

"A real man wouldn't offer his hand," I hear that deep, dark voice behind us. I turn to see Tristan standing there.

"What would he do?" Ben questions, obviously knowing who he is.

"Ash, sit back down," Tristan says. I don't know why I do it but I drop back onto the step and watch as he walks down and steps in front of me. He leans in, his lips so close to my ear, his breath fanning over my cheek before he wraps his arms up under mine and lifts me off the steps with ease. He lets my body slide down the front of his, touching in places we have no business touching.

"That's how you lift a lady," he says, still mere inches from my face. Ben quickly snatches me back to his side, and Tristan lets out a chuckle.

"I don't like you."

"And that should bother me?" Tristan asks him.

"Maybe. Because you're going to be seeing a whole lot of me around, seeing as I'm her boyfriend."

"Oh, I didn't know she had a boyfriend," Tristan says but doesn't move to step back away from us. "You would be smart to keep this one on a leash."

"What does that mean?"

"It means someone might like putting a collar on this one and forcing her to be his little pet."

"You're disgusting," Ben snaps at him. A collar? He can't be serious, right? People don't do that, do they?

"I'm the definition of the word, church boy. She would look really good on a leash, though, wouldn't she?" he taunts, eyeing me up and down. I feel my body shiver, and I don't know why, maybe because he's being so nasty right now.

"I'm warning you. You might be staying in the same house as her, but you won't touch her or disrespect her," Ben tells him, standing up for me.

"I think the lady can speak for herself about what she wants. And I can honestly stand here and tell you that if she ever came to me and asked me to fuck her tight little bible-thumping body, I'd do it."

Ben snarls and steps around me to get to Tristan, fisting his shirt in his hands.

"Stop! He's just trying to make you hit him, Ben. Don't stoop that low," I tell him, grabbing his arm and trying my best to pull him back.

"Yeah, Ben. Don't stoop to the devil." Tristan laughs, but Ben releases the hold he has on him and steps back next to me. He adjusts his shirt for lack of something better to do with his hands before grabbing mine and spinning us to walk away.

He leads me down the sidewalk, and I can't help but turn my head and look over my shoulder at Tristan. He keeps watching us, no watching me. I narrow my eyes at him, but all he does is make a kissing motion with his lips. I quickly turn back and watch where I'm walking.

"I don't like you being in the same house as him. Maybe we should just get married," Ben says.

"What? No. Neither of us are ready for that, Ben, and we're not even engaged."

"We could be. It would get you out of that house of horrors with him." Now I laugh a little.

"It's not going to be that bad. His mom is super nice, and Dad, well, he's Dad. He'll handle things if Tristan gets out of line," I assure him.

"I don't know, Ash. I don't like this."

"It's going to be fine. I promise. Change the subject," I tell him.

"To what? That guy has worked my nerves over now."

"What about the bible camp?"

"What about it? I don't know if I'm going."

"What? Why?" I ask as I stop walking and turn to face him.

"That back there," he says, pointing in the direction of the house. "I don't feel right leaving you there."

"It's my house, Ben. I'll be fine."

"I don't know, Ash."

"Ben, seriously. You've been looking forward to this for a long time. Don't let him get under your skin. I know he isn't getting under mine." He nods his head, but I don't know what he's thinking right now. I have too much at stake to get in the middle of a mess with the likes of Tristan. I have school, and there's no way I'm letting someone like him get in the way of that. It's far too important to me.

"You're probably right. I've just been on edge lately, and I don't like it."

"Why? What's going on?" He looks down at me, and I already know what it is. I won't say a thing to him because it's nothing for him to worry over. I shake my head and raise my hand to stop whatever might be coming out of his mouth next.

"It's fine. Don't think about that," I remind him once more as if I haven't reminded him a million other times.

"It's not. It's very cultish, Ash."

"No, it's not. Is it old school? Yes, it is, but it's not cultish." Ben shakes his head, and I know this bothers him, but there's nothing we can do right now. I have to follow and obey the Lord's word, and that's exactly what I'm going to do.

"I still don't like it."

"It doesn't matter. Nothing matters but us, right?" I ask him when he throws his arm around my shoulder and pulls me into his side.

"You're right. And when I come back from camp, we're getting engaged. I want you out of that house as soon as possible."

"Ben-" I start to argue that we aren't ready for that, but he doesn't listen.

"No. I mean it. We're getting engaged. Maybe not married right away, but the sooner we're engaged, the better." I sigh, wondering if he might be right.

"Okay. But don't bring this up to anyone until after okay?"

"I wouldn't do that. I have some planning to do," he chuckles as we walk down the block. We turn around and head back to the house when I hear the loud music. I look up at Ben before looking toward the small

14

basement window. That's where I see Tristan with a paintbrush.

"I don't even want to know," I mumble as Ben walks me up the steps and closer to the door.

"You sure about this?"

"I'm fine, Ben. I promise." He leans in and kisses my cheek, and I smile in return. I watch him walk back to the driveway to his car before I head inside.

Curiosity gets the better of me, and I walk over, open the basement door, and slowly descend the steps. When I reach the bottom, I see him. Shirtless with a paintbrush in hand. The music was so loud he didn't hear me come down.

I watch as he angrily paints the walls black. I listen to his music but there's so much screaming I can't make out the words, not that it matters. I'm drawn to him. And then I see the fallen angel tattoo that covers his whole back.

My lips part as I take in all the lines and shading. My eyes move from him to the exact painting on the wall. My eyes roam over the painting, and I don't think I've ever seen anything like it. The detail, the colors.

I'm lost in the painting, and I can't seem to find my way out.

"See something you like?" I scream when I hear his voice so close to me. Tristan reaches up and covers my mouth with his hand, and only then do I realize the music has been turned off and all the lights are on.

"You going to scream again?" he asks me. I shake my head, and he slowly moves his hand from my mouth. "You're in my space."

"Did you ... did you paint that?" He looks over his shoulder as if he doesn't know what I'm talking about before looking back at me.

"Yeah. So?"

"That's ... I've never seen anything like that."

"That's kind of the point," he tells me.

"You're very talented. They said you sculpted, but I didn't know you painted, too."

"Does that impress you, Little Nun?" he asks, stepping closer to me. I can feel the heat coming off him, and it suffocates me.

"It's ... intriguing, is all."

"Hmm. That's all?"

"What do you want me to say?" I ask him, looking up at those dark eyes of his.

"Nothing. Get out of my space," he orders, nodding toward the stairs.

"Would you paint me something if I paid you?" He laughs now. It's a loud, dark laugh.

"Hell no."

16

"Why?"

"You think I'm going to paint your Godly shit? You want a pretty little cross with a rose?" he taunts me. I shake my head and step back away from him, heading for the stairs and rushing up them. As I close the door, I hear the music come back on.

I rest my back against the door and close my eyes, willing the visions of him to go away.

"Ash?"

"Yes?"

"Time to pray," my dad calls out. A small wince escapes me before I right myself and walk up to my room.

Chapter 3
Tristan

Oh, Little Nun. Little does she know I've been down here painting her all fucking day. I can't get her face out of my head, and that's a bad, bad thing. I know I can't touch her. I don't want to either, but fuck is she gorgeous and tempting as hell.

I spin the painting around and set it back up on my easel, then step back and take a look at it. It's perfect. Same pouty lips. Same dark hair. Same face I want to ruin, but I won't. Mom's happy, and that's all I could ask for. That's all I ever wanted for her. A religious husband? Yeah, that wasn't on my bingo card, but as long as he treats her right, that's all I care about, and so far, he has.

I stare at her picture far longer than I should before putting the finishing touches on it. A little black rose in her hand, and it's complete.

I see Ash. I see she's hiding things from everyone around her. I would know a wounded soul when I see one. I've had one for a very long time.

I finish what I'm doing and clean up before grabbing a shirt and heading up the stairs. I lock the basement door behind me so no one goes down there and sees what I've done. It's none of their fucking business.

I head out the door, grab my helmet, jump on my bike, and take off. I weave through the streets and down the back alleys to get to the party. When I arrive, I'm greeted by my best friend, Rod.

"You made it."

"Don't I always," I tell him. He laughs, and we fist bump before I follow him inside. This weekend is all about having fun, and that's exactly what I'm going to do.

We walk down the dark staircase until we reach the bottom. That's where the party picks up. Lights are flashing, people are dancing, and the music is thumping. It's not my typical music, but I like all kinds.

I follow Rod to the back, where a few of our other friends sit and join them.

"How's the married life?" Andy chuckles.

"I wouldn't know. They aren't married yet. Two weeks. But the house is pretty nice," I reply.

"Not with you in it," Rod adds, causing me to laugh.

"Already started on the basement," I tell him.

"No shit? What'd you paint?"

"The same thing." They all know my love of fallen angels.

"So, the new sister?" Andy asks as he passes me the joint. I bring it to my lips and inhale.

"She isn't bad looking. Bible thumper," I answer.

"No fucking way."

"Oh yeah. Her dad is big time into that shit."

"And you're the unholy one," he adds, causing me to laugh once more.

"Something like that." I sit back and pass a joint around as the music keeps playing. Eventually, we order some drinks and the night truly gets going. The only time I truly feel free of my demons is when I'm drunk and high. I know a lot of people use that as an excuse, but not me. It's the truth.

I tip my head back when I feel hands on my thighs, and when I lift my head and look down, I see Amber on her knees between my legs.

"Long time no suck," she says as she smiles up at me.

"By all means." I motion to my hardening cock. She licks her lips and unzips my jeans, and I lift to help her get them down. Then she's licking the tip of my cock before sucking it down her throat.

Amber and I have a strange relationship, if that's what you'd even call it. We fuck around but with no strings attached. I guess it's that friends with benefits shit people are always talking about. For me? She's a fuck when I need it. Like now. Because all I can think about is those light brown fucking eyes and those pouty lips.

I groan as Ash's face flashes in my head. My doc is going to have a fun time with this one. You see, I become obsessed with things. Things I can't control and I have a bad feeling Ash is going to be one of those things.

Amber keeps bobbing her head up and down, and I groan as she takes me deep into her throat. She reaches up and grabs my balls in her hand, and that's about all I can deal with right now. I shoot my cum down the back of her throat, watching her as she gags to try and swallow it all. I almost feel bad for her, almost.

Instead, I keep fucking coming, and she keeps fucking taking. When she's done, she pulls back and lifts her skirt.

"In a minute," I tell her knowing she wants my cock inside her. She huffs out a breath and turns to walk away, and I let her. I don't need her on me right this minute.

"You turned her down?"

"She just sucked my cock. She'll be fine." Andy laughs harder.

"You're so fucked. So, what's been up with you besides the move? Haven't seen you around much," Andy says.

"Been busy with work. You should see the fucking sculpture I'm working on now. The guy even gave me a fucking nude model to sculpt."

"You're shitting me?" I shake my head.

"Nope. She's hot, too. Not my type, but still, she has a nice fucking body on her. This sculpture is going to come out great," I tell him.

"They all do. In fact, my dad wants to talk to you about doing one for him."

"Of what? Satan?" I chuckle.

"Probably some sick shit like that. You against it?" he asks, and I shake my head once more.

"Fuck no. I'd love to sculpt that. Just have him call me." He nods his head, passes another joint around, and I grab it in my fingers.

"Shit," Rod hisses from next to me. I turn my head to see what he's pissed about when I see him. I start to shove out of my chair, but Rod shoves me back down.

"Let him come over here first, Tristan."

"Fuck him. He shouldn't even be here. Why is he here?" I ask, anger evident in my tone.

"I don't know. He knows no one wants him around." We watch as he fists bumps a few people before turning his gaze on us. I pass the joint off to Andy and crack my knuckles, ready for this fight.

The punk, Shane, starts toward us with a smile on his ugly face. When he's close enough I stand and watch as he walks over.

"What do you want?"

"To party like everyone else."

"This isn't your place, Shane."

"Come on, Tristan. Let that shit go." I glance over at Andy and Rod, smiling as I drag my gaze back to Shane's.

Then, before he has the chance to respond or move, I swing. I punch the fucker right in the jaw, causing him to stumble back into Rod. Rod shoves him back in my direction, and I hit the bastard again. He starts to fight back, hitting me. I'm ready for the fight. I've waited a long time for this day.

Fists fly before we're pulled apart. I know it's the club's security, but with all the beef we have with this prick, I know they won't bother me. When we're forced apart, they stare him down.

"You don't belong here," One of them tells him as I smirk at him.

"Didn't I tell you that?" I ask him.

"Fuck you, Tristan! This isn't over."

"Not until your hot blood is spilled all over my hands, it isn't. You got that part right," I warn him.

"You think you can kill me?" He sneers at me.

"You think you could kill Jimmy and not have that shit come back on you? There's a place and a fucking time, Shane. And your time is coming." I can see the anger in his eyes, but he knows this shit isn't over, not by a long shot. He took a life, and the only way to repay that is by taking his. But with everything, the time has to be right.

I can't draw too much attention to myself, and I don't. I keep a low profile and do what needs to be done, and just like with all things, this is worth waiting for.

The security drags his ass out of the club as we all watch and grin at him. He's pissed, we can all see it, but he killed a good friend of ours, and I'll repay that debt at some point.

"Fuck, I can't believe he showed up here," Rod grumbles as I grab another beer and bring it to my lips.

"Me either. Stupid fuck."

"He's going to get what's coming, Tristan."

"I know he is. By my fucking hands."

"We're all here to help with that shit," Andy adds.

"No. He's mine and mine alone. I've never wanted something so bad in my goddamn life," I tell the two of them.

The night wears on, and the more I smoke, the more I want to fly. There's something wrong in this head of mine. Has been for a long time. No one can figure me out. No one knows what it is. I've been sent to specialists when I was younger, and they have done all kinds of sick shit to me. Every test, every trial, and nothing. I'm a rarity. An oddity. A mystery no one can decipher, and to be honest? I don't mind it. I love being me and who the fuck I am.

Chapter 4
Ash

"Come on, Ash. Live a little," Annie, one of my friends, encourages me.

"It's someone's car!"

"And? We're going to track you the whole time."

"What if they find me in there first and murder me?" I ask her with a slight laugh.

"No one is going to find you."

"We're on the worst side of town, Annie. My dad is already going to have a fit if he finds out," I remind her and myself. I'm praying to God he doesn't find out, and I'm also praying for forgiveness.

"I did it last time, and I was fine," she reminds me. Her idea of fun is getting into some stranger's car without them knowing and letting them drive to wherever it is they're going, then having friends pick us up. We make sure we're tracking each other before we do it, and honestly, I know just how dangerous it is, but I love the little thrill and butterflies I get when they do it. I've never done it yet, but they all have.

"Okay, fine. Which car," I ask. Annie and Ginger both look around before picking one.

"That one." I nod my head, and we sync our phones before I sneak over and test the trunk. The SUV opens easily, and I slide in, lying down so I can't be seen. I pull the door shut behind me and that's where I stay until I hear someone opening both the driver and passenger doors. They both slam shut, and I clench my eyes shut as the car starts up and we pull out. I look down at the screen of my phone and lower the light levels so they won't be able to see the glow.

My heart is pounding against my ribs as music plays, but no one speaks. The ride doesn't seem to take long, and before I know it, the engine dies, and they climb out. I wait a few minutes with my heart rapping against my ribcage until I feel it's safe to climb out. When I do, I glance around but don't see Ginger and Annie here yet.

I look over and notice it's an old warehouse. I walk closer and see there's a small window with no covering over it, so I peek inside. That's when I see him.

Tristan.

There's a girl on top of him, riding him, some sort of clamps on her nipples that link to a chain he keeps pulling, and her lips keep parting. I know I shouldn't be watching this, but I can't help myself. I'm drawn to him in ways I know I shouldn't, but Tristan is intriguing. His muscles move when she presses her nails into his chest and slowly drags them over his body. I can see the angry red marks from here.

Do people actually like this? Is this what sex is? I wouldn't know since I've never done it, but now I'm curious. I keep watching as she bounces on him harder and faster. His hands move around her waist and hold her there, stilling her. You can tell she isn't happy about it either, judging by the pout on her face.

He's saying something and smiling up at her, but she doesn't look happy about it. Finally, he lets go and slaps a hand on her thigh multiple times until you can visibly see the red outline of his palm. I gasp and cover my mouth.

This can't be right. This can't be how having sex is, is it? I keep watching even as he turns his head with his eyes closed. I should move away from the window, but I don't. It's like I'm stuck in place, and I can't move. And do I really want to? My cheeks heat as I watch what they're doing, but it's not until I hear the horn behind me that I know Ginger and Annie are here. I start to pull my eyes away from the scene in front of me, but when I look up at his face once more, I see him staring right back at me.

He doesn't make a move to stop her. He doesn't make a move or say anything. His eyes linger on mine, and heat coils inside of me. Heat I've never felt before. I don't know how or why I feel like this, but after one more beep, I pull my gaze away from him and rush to the car. I climb in, my breathing coming sporadically.

"Are you okay?" Annie asks.

"Yeah. That was crazy."

"Who was it? Some drug dealer?" she asks. I shrug as she takes off down the road, glancing over my shoulder to see if he came out. He didn't.

"I think I need water," I tell her. Annie nods, and we pull over at a local diner and climb out. We head inside and then sit, ordering something to drink.

"So? What was your person like?"

"They played really loud music, and no one spoke the whole way," I tell them. It's true.

"What? They didn't even talk? That's so weird," Annie adds as I take down my water and ask for more. The two of them stare at me and I wonder if they can sense what I was doing. No, there's no way.

"What's going on? Are you okay?"

"Yeah. I'm just really thirsty for some reason," I tell them. When the waitress sets down the next glass, I grab that one, too.

"What did you see in there?" Ginger asks this time.

"Nothing. I'm okay, really. I think I was just hot in that trunk."

"Anyways. So Ben is leaving soon. What are you going to do with your time?" Annie asks me, changing the subject thankfully.

"I was thinking of volunteering at the youth center while he's gone. You know, the arts and craft department always need help."

"That would be fun, and since you're studying art, that works out great for you."

"I can't imagine how hard it is to keep helpers there. I mean, it's on the worst side of town, but I think I can do a lot of good there."

"Oh, I know you can. You're so good with kids, and you love what you do. I think that's great," Annie says.

"I wish you would do something more spontaneous."

"Like what?"

"I don't know. I can't really think of anything off the top of my head, but you're always so predictable."

"There's nothing wrong with that," Annie chimes in.

"No, but look how long it took us to get her to play our little game," she adds.

"Your little game isn't safe. I don't even know why we're having this conversation."

"Because you're a little stuck up, Ash." I gasp at her words. I thought we were friends. Apparently, I was wrong. I stand and leave the table with Annie calling out to me. I raise my hand over my shoulder so she can stop and storm out of the diner. I know this area isn't the safest, but I have my mace my dad gave me and instead of calling him and getting in trouble, I turn off my location on my phone and start walking. I can't believe she said that to me.

29

I keep walking even as the chill of the night hits me. Cars blow past me, blaring their horn until one pulls up next to me. I start to panic, not knowing what to do. I reach into my pocket and pull out my mace, ready to spray and run if I have to.

"What the hell is that?" I hear Tristan's voice from the other side of the car.

"Mace."

"What are you going to do with it?"

"I didn't know it was you," I retort, still holding tightly to it. He stalks around the car and stops in front of me, staring me down.

"You going to use it?" he asks, nodding toward the mace in my hand.

"Do I need to?" He lets out a laugh that sends heat spiraling inside of me. Again, this feeling is new to me, and I don't know what it means.

"I think you're safe, Little Nun. Get in the car," he says, nodding toward the SUV. I walk over, and he opens the door, ushering me inside. When I climb in, he closes the door and walks around to get in. Once he's in, he turns to me and grins. He doesn't speak, just smiles. Then he's turning back to the front and taking off.

We drive to where I climbed into the back of the SUV, and he parks.

"What are we doing?"

"I need to get my bike. This isn't my car," he tells me.

"Bike?"

"Motorcycle," he says as he climbs out and motions for me to do the same. I keep my hand in my pocket, wrapped around my mace, ready to spray it at a moment's notice. "Come on, Little Nun." I follow behind him down a set of stairs and into what appears to be a club. There are people everywhere, and I cough from the smoke filling the room. I watch as Tristan tosses the keys to someone and then grabs another set. All eyes turn to me as I stand in the corner near the door, ready to bolt at any second.

"Let's go," Tristan says when he walks back over to me. We climb the stairs once more and then head back out toward his bike.

"I'll call a taxi."

"No, you won't."

"Yeah, I think I will."

"No, Little Nun. I think you fucking won't. I'm taking your ass home."

"What if my dad is there?"

"Then you can tell him how we came about riding home together," he taunts.

"I … I can't do that."

"I'll drop you off down the street. Get on," he demands, passing me a helmet. I slide it on my head and climb on the bike after him. I grab his jacket and hold onto it, but he just laughs.

"You'll be out of control, Ash. You have to hold onto me."

"What? No."

"Yeah, Ash. Either that or you're going to kill us both. You ready to meet your maker?" he asks me. I shake my head, and he grabs my hands, pulling them around his waist. This is wrong. It's so wrong, and I know it, but what am I supposed to do? I hold onto him as he revs the bike engine and takes off.

We hit the road and I can almost feel myself start to relax into him. I've never felt anything like this, being on the back of his bike. I've never felt so at ease or so free. It's the strangest feeling in the world but I find I like it.

We pull onto our street and just like he said, he pulls over to let me off.

"Thank you."

"Why are you smiling?" he asks, keeping his tone even.

"I've never been on a bike before."

"Clearly. So that's why you're smiling?"

"It was amazing, Tristan. Thank you." He shakes his head as I pass him the helmet I had on. He slips it on his head and nods toward the house, wanting me to go. I start walking, and I can feel him behind me, watching my every move.

When I make it to the house, he revs up the bike and takes off down the road passing me altogether.

Chapter 5
Tristan

He thinks this scares me. This twisted, sick fuck of a doctor. It doesn't. There's no fear in me anymore. None I can feel anyway. So when I hear the click of the gun against my temple, I don't even flinch. Over and over again, he does this. Mock execution is a form of psychological torture. The piece of shit doctor thinks he can scare me straight, but all I can do is laugh in his face. He doesn't appreciate that much, though.

"This isn't working."

"Clearly," he responds, pulling the hood off my head.

"What was the point?"

"I don't know anymore, Tristan. Scaring you straight? Something has to work, right?"

"The meds don't work. Talking doesn't work. Your scare tactics are laughable. I'm a fucking lost cause, Doc." He sighs, and I stand, offering my tied arms to him to untie. He does, and we walk over, sitting back on the couch as usual.

"Why don't we talk about my newest obsession."

"Which is?" he asks.

"My new little stepsister."

"No."

"No?"

"No, Tristan. Do you understand the severity of your condition?"

"Considering you have no fucking clue what's wrong with me? No."

"Yes, you do. Remember the last time you became obsessed with a girl?"

"I was ten, you stupid fuck!"

"And she ended up dead, Tristan," he reminds me. He's not wrong. We were playing a game, a game of life, and she hung herself. Of course, I was blamed for it, but I was younger back then, and there wasn't much they could do with me. I was locked up in a mental institute for three years before they released me to my mom.

The professionals say I can't love. They say I can't hate, and I can't feel. But they're all fucking wrong because I can feel all of those emotions. I choose not to, of course. Why should I? Why should I feel anything for anyone when I don't have to? But this? This thing with Ash? It's different, and I know it.

"Semantics."

"Is it? You can't become obsessed with this girl, Tristan. It will only end badly for both of you. I know there are some sort of feelings deep down inside of you that you chose to suppress, and I can understand why you may think you're obsessed with this girl, but you're not. She's just another girl."

"Is she? Just another girl, that is."

"Yes, she is. You have to put your focus on something else, Tristan. Your work, for example. I hear great things about your work." I nod my head. There are always good things to say about my work. I'm fucking great at what I do.

"Focus on work, huh?" I ask as I sit back and light a cigarette. The Doc doesn't care if I smoke in here, and I take full advantage of that.

"Yes. Your work will be seen all over the world one day," he tells me, causing me to laugh.

"You're shitting me, right? No one gives two fucks about me, Doc. The work? Yes, but when it comes down to the artist, they all fucking agree to keep me anonymous for a reason."

"They fear you."

"As they should," I tell him, leaning forward, resting my elbows on my knees. I point my fingers at him before I begin to speak again. "They're afraid of what I am. Of what I create and what I can do to them."

"What can you do?"

"Come on, Doc. You've known me for twenty-two years. I think you know what I'm capable of."

"But will you follow through?"

"When have I not?" The bell sounds, letting me know my session is over. I snuff out my cigarette and stand from the couch, mock saluting his ass before heading out the door.

My mom waits outside, just like always. This is our time together. I give it to her weekly because I know she worries about me, and that's the last thing I want.

"How'd it go?"

"He wants me to focus on my work more."

"I'd agree. You're doing really great things with your art, Tristan. In fact, I've been asked to speak to you about helping out down at the youth center."

"What the fuck?" I laugh now. "Me at the youth center? I don't fucking think so."

"Really? You don't want to help others who may be like you?" she asks.

"There's no one like me, mom. I'm the sole fucking devil."

"Tristan, come on. I hear Ash is going to work down there a bit. Maybe you two could go together." Now, that has piqued my interest. If Ash is going, that would give me more time around her, which is exactly what I need.

"She is? She's a little fucking do-gooder, isn't she?" I laugh.

"No. Her dad has raised her to be there and help others."

"You know I'm sorry."

37

"For what?"

"Not being the perfect son."

"You're perfect in your own way, Tristan. You know that. We've been over this," she tells me, reaching over to rest her hand on mine. I nod my head, although I don't really feel shit.

"Youth center, huh?"

"Yeah. Could be fun."

"Doubtful."

"You'll think about it? For me?"

"For you, I will." She smiles happily before pulling out onto the road. We make it back to the house, and I head inside when I hear her soft sobs. I walk down the hall and see her bedroom door open and her on her knees on a broomstick. I'm about to speak and say something when her dad steps in front of me. He smiles like this is normal and closes the door in my face. What the fuck is he doing to her?

Ignoring the nagging in the back of my mind telling me to fuck his world up and grab her, I head for the basement instead.

I strip out of my shirt and grab the paint, popping it open, and get back to work on the walls down here. Fucking white. I can't stand white walls. There's just something so depressing about them. I know most would say that about black, but that's not how I see it.

I finish painting and turn on some music, grabbing a joint and lighting a few candles around the room. Then I sit back and smoke, thinking about what the Doc and what my mom said. One trying to keep me away from the girl the other pushing me toward her. I chuckle at the irony of them both.

I keep smoking until I hear the door slam and a car take off out of the driveway. I walk over to the small window and peer out to see Ted's car gone.

Snuffing out my joint, I walk up the steps and straight toward her room. The doors open, and I can hear soft sobs coming from inside. When I shove the door the rest of the way, I get a view of her naked back.

"He fucking do that to you?" She jumps, covering herself before grabbing a shirt and pulling it on.

"It's a sin to see my naked flesh, Tristan."

"Isn't it a sin for him to beat on you?" I can feel the anger, my demons simultaneously rattling their cages inside me from seeing the marks on her flesh.

"I am to obey, and I didn't."

"What the hell could you have done wrong, Little Nun?"

"He found out I was out the other night," she replies softly.

"The night you watched me?" I ask her. Now she turns, her eyes shooting to mine.

"You can't tell him."

"Why would I? I think I liked having your eyes on me. Seeing my naked fucking flesh," I tell her. Ash's cheeks turn pink as she looks anywhere but at me. I step into her room and I can feel her tremble from here. I don't even need to be touching her. I reach out and lift her chin so she has to look at me.

"Did you like it?"

"What?"

"What you saw. Did you like watching her riding me? Did you get wet?"

"I … I don't …"

"Hmm. You know what it feels like, Little Nun? The way your heart kicks up a notch, your breathing speeds up. The wetness pooling between those pretty little thighs of yours." Fuck I can nearly smell her arousal from here. The way her cheeks turn pink tells me I'm getting to her.

"You need to leave."

"Do you touch yourself at night thinking about me?"

"I do no such thing!" She tries to pull her face from me, but I hold on tighter this time.

"If you want me to handle your dad, just say the words."

"What do you mean?"

"He has no right to hurt you, Little Nun. I'm pretty sure the Bible says otherwise." She snorts a laugh, and I release her face and step back.

"What do you know about the Bible?"

"I know enough."

"Get out."

"No. I like being in your unholy space."

"My space isn't unholy."

"It is when you're letting him hurt you. You know who should be hurting you? Me. That should be my marks on your flesh."

"What are you talking about?" Now, I step back into her space, crowding her as she backs against the wall.

"I like to mark what's mine, Ash. And I've got this crazy as hell idea in my head you are mine."

"You're right. It's crazy. I'm not yours."

"But you are. Up here," I say, tapping my fingers against my temple. "You're up here, and there's no fucking getting you out. Do you realize how frustrating that is for me?"

"What are you talking about, Tristan?"

"I'm not all here," I tell her, tapping my temple again. "In fact, I'm not right in my head, and the fact I have this new fucking obsession with you is a problem, Ash."

"Why would you be obsessed with me?" her bottom lip trembles when she speaks, and I can feel my cock hardening in my jeans.

"Because it always ends badly for one of us."

"You've done this before?"

"When I was younger."

"And what happened to her?" I debate telling her what happened. To that little girl who caught all my fucking attention back then.

"She's dead." Ash gasps loudly and tries to move, but I cage her in with my arms, resting my hands on the wall on either side of her head.

"Get away from me."

"Is that what you really want?" I ask her. She nods her head, but I don't hear any words coming from her mouth, so I take that as my reason to stay exactly where I am.

"Take your panties off," I tell her. She narrows her eyes and shakes her head. "Now, or I'll do it for you, Ash." I step back enough for her to move, and when I do, she tries to run. I reach out and grab her around the waist, slamming her against the wall where she was just at. "I'll do it."

"Please don't."

"Then do it, Ash!" I roar at her. She reaches down and slips her hands under her skirt, pulling her panties off and holding them tightly in her hand. "Now give them to me."

Slowly, she puts them in the palm of my outstretched hand. I close my fist around them before bringing them to my nose and inhaling, closing my eyes. If I weren't a fucking obsessed man before, I would be now.

I open my eyes and look at Ash before nodding my head and stepping back, letting her go. She takes off into her bathroom, shutting the door when I hear the lock click into place. I smile, knowing I'm getting to her the same fucking way she's getting under my fucking skin.

Chapter 6
Ash

I should feel degraded, except I don't. I almost feel empowered. Like I can take on the world after what he did to me. I should be ashamed, yet strangely, I'm not. I know deep down I'll regret doing that. I know if my dad finds out what I did, he'll beat me until I can't walk for my sins.

It's been a few days and no one seems to notice the strange tension between me and Tristan. We had a family dinner that, of course, Tristan made uncomfortable for me.

Now, I'm intrigued more than anything. I walk down the stairs to find him much the same as the last time, painting.

"What's that?" He quickly turns to look at me, blocking his painting from my sight.

"None of your concern."

"Who's your favorite painter?" I ask, hoping to gain some insight into Tristan because he's very closed off.

"Again, none of your business."

"I study art in college. I want to teach," I tell him, praying that maybe he'll join the conversation.

"Teach?"

"Yeah, art classes for kids. That's my dream."

"That's a bullshit dream, Little Nun. You can do more than that."

"Such as?"

"Be my little whore. On your knees praying to me every night," he says, his eyes as black as coal. I can feel the heat in my cheeks, and I know he can see it.

"There's nothing wrong with my dream. Don't you have dreams?"

"No. I have nightmares."

"Can I look at your paintings?"

"Listen, I don't know what the fuck you're trying to do here but stop. We're not the same, Ash. We don't have the same fucking interests or the same goals here. Whatever you're thinking … don't."

"I want more."

"More what?"

"Out of life, Tristan. I feel like I've been locked in a cage my whole life and know nothing about the real world."

"You don't know shit about the real world. You're right about that," Tristan confirms as he runs his hand through his hair.

"I just want to learn more."

"Then ask your dad." He dismisses me, turning his back on me, and that makes me angry. I don't know why I want Tristan to show me his world so badly, but I do.

"I have shit to do," he says before grabbing a shirt and walking up the stairs. I follow him up the stairs and outside, where he jumps on his bike. I climb into my car, and I follow him. I don't know why I'm doing this or what's going to happen, but I just want to live in the moment. His moment.

He takes a ton of turns, stops at a few places, and I wait it out to see what he's doing, but he always comes back with nothing. I have no idea what he's doing in there but I want to know.

I wasn't lying when I said I was sheltered my whole life. All I know is what the Bible says and what it teaches or what my dad says to me.

I shift in my seat and wince at the pain in my back where I was hit with a stick for not following the rules, and I go back to what Tristan said that day. Did I really deserve that? Is that what the bible is telling him to do to me? Why? What did I do that was so bad? I was exploring life a little more than I usually do.

I find myself losing track of Tristan since he's on his bike and driving faster than me so I pull over at a store downtown and climb out. I walk inside and I know right away that this isn't the type of store I should be in. Nothing in here is remotely close to what I wear, but the more I look around, the more intrigued I become.

"Can I help you?" A small girl with pink hair walks over and asks me. I smile, loving how it looks on her.

"I like your hair."

"Thanks. Did you need something?" she asks as she looks me up and down.

"If I was looking for something different than what I have on, what would you suggest?" She eyes me once more before smiling.

"Basically, anything in the store, but I'm assuming you don't want to go too crazy, right?"

"Exactly."

"Come with me." I follow her through the store as she grabs a pair of jeans with a few tiny rips in them and a black t-shirt. Then she leads me to the changing room, where she places the clothes on the hook.

"They should fit. If not, let me know," she tells me as I step in and pull the curtain closed. I hurriedly pull off my long skirt and shirt and slide into the jeans. I've never worn a pair of jeans before. Ever. Not as far back as I can remember. Having them on feels different, and I like it. I turn to face the mirror and a tear slides down my cheek.

"This is going against God, isn't it?" I ask more to myself.

"No, it's not." The curtain pulls back, and the girl steps in and looks at me. "You're super religious?"

"I was raised that way. I've never worn jeans," I admit as she reaches up and wipes the tear from my cheek.

"I was raised that way too. I let it all go a long time ago. I'm happy now. I have a life that isn't dictated by them. I still believe in God but I don't have to live my life by their rules."

"You still believe?"

"Yeah. I'm not insane. I just found what worked for me," she laughs.

"How much for the clothes?"

"Those are on me. Come back when you want more, and I'll hook you up. I'm Cher."

"I'm Ash. Thank you so much for this."

"Anytime you want to talk. When you're ready, I'll give you my number." She smiles at me before stepping out of the dressing room and leaving me alone to gather my thoughts. I gather my clothes and head to the register, where she gives me a bag for my old ones and her number. As I walk out of the store, a new sense of confidence engulfs me. I've never felt like this. Never had this much self-esteem. I think I like it.

I hop back in the car and just drive around with a huge smile on my face. I'm sure if anyone saw me, they would think I was crazy, but I don't care right now. I'm living in the moment.

Taking the risk, I drive over to where I saw Tristan at that warehouse, but I don't see his bike. I park the car and climb out, heading to the door to see if it's unlocked, and strangely, it is. I step inside, close the door behind me, and start to wander.

Just like at home, the walls are black, and there are paintings hung everywhere. Mostly of fallen angels, which intrigues me.

I keep looking around until I hear him clear his throat.

Chapter 7
Tristan

I press my tongue into the side of my cheek as I look at her. She's afraid, I can tell. Hell, I can practically smell the fear coming off her. She's dressed differently, almost like me, in dark-colored clothes I would have never thought I'd see her in.

I stand here with my knife in one hand, pressing it into the tip of my finger as she watches the blood slowly bloom on the surface and then eventually drop to the floor.

"I should go," she whispers.

"You should stay," I tell her. She shakes her head as she looks around the room for a way to escape, but there isn't one. She'd have to go through me first, and I don't think she's willing to do that.

"I think I'll go," she repeats.

"Why are you here?"

"I … I just want to leave," she murmurs, but I shake my head this time. She isn't going anywhere until I get the answers I want. She starts toward the door, but I step in front of it to block it.

"You know what I think?" I ask her, pressing the tip of my knife into my temple. "I think you like me."

"I don't like you. You're ... strange."

"Intriguing?"

"No. Just strange."

"Is that a Godly thing to say about someone?" I ask, taunting her.

"It's a statement."

"Hmm. I suppose it is. So, back to my original question. What are you doing here?"

"I made a mistake."

"Such as?"

"Why are you questioning me? Just let me leave," she nearly demands. I pull the knife from my temple and point it at her, watching her wince as I do.

"You came into my space when I wasn't here. You came into my fucking lair, and you think you're just going to walk back out of it? I don't think so, Little Nun."

"Tristan, just let me go."

"Why are you here?" I roar louder this time, watching the way she jolts. She's afraid for her safety, that I'm sure of, but now isn't the time for fear. Now is the time for fun.

"I was just looking around."

"At what?"

"Your stuff."

"So you broke into my space just to look at my stuff? Tsk tsk, Little Nun."

"I'm sorry. You're right. I shouldn't have done it." She steps toward the door, and I smirk at her, holding the knife out toward her.

"You're not leaving until I say you can. Now get on your knees."

"What? No," she instantly says, shaking her head.

"You want to leave? You're going to do as I say," I tell her.

"Or I could yell."

"Who's going to come and rescue you? There's no one here," I remind her. She looks between me and the door, and something stops her from trying to leave again. Maybe it's the fact she knows there's no one here to help her. Or maybe it's because she's still fucking intrigued by me, and she wants to know more. Either way is fine by me.

"On. Your. Knees." I tell her once more. Ash licks her lips before sliding to the floor on her knees, and fuck me, does she look nothing but perfect like this. At my mercy. Cock level. A groan leaves my throat as I step toward her.

"Raise your hand and grab my cock," I order her.

"No," she states firmly. She starts to stand up once more, and I stop her with the knife. I press it to her cheek hard enough she feels it but not hard enough to draw blood.

"No? Are you in charge right now, Little Nun? Grab my fucking cock." I press the tip in just slightly harder, and she winces but raises her hand to rest it on my cock. Her hand feels so fucking good right there.

I bring my other hand over and rest it on top of hers before forcing her to rub it. She tries to pull back, but I don't let her.

"You can either rub it like this, or I can pull it out for you," I tell her. Her eyes shoot up to mine, and I know I'll never get the look of her on her knees in front of me out of my fucking head. It's cemented there forever.

I groan as the two of us rub my cock, that motherfucker wants more than just her hand, but for now, this is going to do.

I rock my hips into our hands, squeezing hers around my cock.

"You're going to make me come, Little Nun."

"Tristan." Is that a plea? Is she begging? Either way, she's going to do it. I'm not about to let her walk away from me without getting me off first.

"Ash."

"Please don't make me do this," she begs as tears fall down her perfect fucking cheeks.

53

"Oh, is it a sin, Little Nun? For you to jerk off your stepbrother? There has to be a first time, right? Otherwise, how are you going to do it later on?" Now, her teary eyes land on mine, and I can see the struggle in them. She doesn't want to do this, but a part deep down inside of her? Oh, she wants me to ruin her. She wants me to take her and fuck her against the cross on her daddy's wall. And when the time comes? I'm going to. I'm going to force her to sin all over that fucking bible ridden house.

"Come on, Ash." The harder I force her to squeeze, the closer I can feel myself getting. I keep us working together as I moan and groan, picturing her lips wrapped around me instead of her hand, but for now, this will do.

"So fucking close," I tell her. Tears keep spilling down her cheeks as I keep the motion going, and then that's it. I can't hold back anymore. I come in my fucking jeans like a little schoolboy, and I don't even care.

"Oh fuck, Little Nun. This is so good," I tell her as I groan. When I'm done, I release her hand to find her cheeks a pretty shade of pink. "Ash? Are you wet right now?"

"What? No."

"Stand up." She stands to her feet and steps closer, resting my hand on her hip and sliding my hand into her pants. Then I slowly slip my hand between her legs, and she trembles.

"Fuck, Little Nun. Are you always this wet when you see me?"

"I'm … I'm not."

"You're going to stand here and lie to my face? Is God going to like you being a little liar? Is he going to like the sinning you're doing right now? You should have never let the Devil touch you, Ash, because now you're going to be ruined and tarnished for life." I lean down and sink my teeth into her shoulder through her shirt and groan as a soft squeal comes from her lips.

"Next time, it'll be bare skin, Ash. Next time, I'm going to taste your flesh as it presses against my lips."

Chapter 8
Ash

His words ring in my head. Ruined and tarnished for life. Maybe he's right. Maybe that's what I am. I messed up. I shouldn't have gone there. I shouldn't have touched him.

I made it home before everyone else and changed my clothes before Ben came over. Now we sit on the porch swing, and I wonder if his private parts are like Tristan's. His was more than a handful.

"What's wrong?" Ben asks when I zone out thinking about Tristan's words to me.

"Nothing. I didn't sleep well last night," I lie to him just as Tristan walks up onto the porch.

"Hey, Sis. How's your day?" he asks, his tone as smug as ever.

"She isn't your sis. Stop calling her that."

"She basically is. The wedding is coming up, and we are going together," Tristan reminds us. I forgot about that. His mom had asked for us to walk down the aisle together, and I suppose it wouldn't be the worst thing in the world.

"Leave her alone."

"Holding hands and things," he taunts, his unspoken innuendo clear as day. My cheeks heat again, and I can feel it.

"You're not touching her."

"How do you want me to walk her down the aisle then?" he asks Ben. Ben shoves off the swing and stands in Tristan's face which probably isn't the best of ideas because that's what Tristan wants.

"If I had my way, you wouldn't be doing anything with her," he snaps. Tristan's eyes move to meet mine and then back to Ben's.

"Come on, bible boy. She's my sister," he tells him, angering Ben even more. I can see his hands clench, and I decide to step into the middle of them. I stand pushing Ben back a step, not that I was worried about him. Ben isn't a small guy, but compared to Tristan, he doesn't stand a chance.

"Just stop. Both of you. Ben, you've known this for a while now," I remind him. He nods his head.

"Doesn't mean I have to like it. Maybe I should stay," he adds.

"No. You're not doing that. You've been planning on attending this camp for a long time now," I tell him.

"Oh yeah, Ben. We wouldn't want you to miss camp. All the thrilling things I'm sure you'll be doing there," Tristan adds. I almost laugh, but I cover it with a cough instead.

"Let's just stop. We're all adults here."

"You're right, Sis. I can't wait to see you in a dress," Tristan says before pulling out a cigarette and lighting it up. Ben growls low in his throat, but Tristan doesn't care. He enjoys his smoke like he never said anything.

"Ben, you need to go. You're going to be late," I tell him. Reluctantly he nods and leans in, pressing a kiss to my cheek. I smile back at him when he turns and walks away, climbing into his car. I watch as he pulls out and takes off down the street.

"Do you get some thrill out of making him mad?"

"That depends."

"On what?"

"Does he hit you like your dad does?" he asks me. His words hurt. They sting, and I shake my head. "Then no. I don't get a fucking thrill out of it, but what I do know is one day, I'm going to make your dad feel the same pain you feel," he informs me before walking down the steps.

"You can't do that!"

"Why not?"

"He's going to be your dad," I tell him. Tristan stiffens before turning and walking the short distance back to me.

"No. He'll never be my dad. I don't need one, never have, and never will. If he so much as lays a hand on me, I'll gut him."

"Tristan, this is the real world. You can't just kill him." He cocks his head to look at me, and in his eyes, I can see all the darkness that consumes his soul. He would do it. He would kill him, and he wouldn't have any remorse for doing it.

"You see me, Ash?"

"I-"

"Do you see me, Ash? The deepest parts of my soul. Can you see it?" he asks me softly. I nod my head, and a sick grin crosses his face. "No. You don't. You see what I let you see. You see what I give everyone. A tiny sliver of fear and darkness in the pits of hell is where I dwell. That's what I let you see, Ash."

"I don't think you're evil, Tristan."

"Oh, but I am. And if you don't stay away from me, you're going to find out just how evil I can be," he tells me, pointing at me with his cigarette still between his fingers. I reach out and take it from him, bringing it to my lips. Tristan cocks his head to the side to stare at me as if I'm crazy. And maybe I am. Maybe I'm turning into a monster.

I inhale and immediately begin to choke on it. Tristan doesn't laugh or make fun of me; he just watches me intently.

"That's very unholy of you."

"When I'm around you, I feel like doing very unholy things."

"Such as?"

"I ..." I can't say it out loud and he knows it. He steps closer, getting into my space before reaching up and taking his cigarette back from me.

"All you have to do is ask, Ash."

"What do you mean?"

"You want something, you ask. That's it."

"I can't just ask."

"Sure you can. Try it."

"I've never … I've never kissed anyone on the lips before." I'm almost too embarrassed to say it, and now here I am saying it to Tristan of all people. He nods his head and takes another drag from his cigarette before blowing the smoke into the air. He steps in, leaning down into my space, and presses his lips against mine.

"Now kiss me back," he demands, his tone dark and firm. I open my mouth, parting my lips, and he begins to work his over mine. I catch on quickly, and we kiss for what seems like a long time, but it could very well only be seconds, I don't know. I'm lost. I feel like I'm floating on a high when I'm around him.

"Did I do it wrong?" I ask him when he suddenly pulls back. He shakes his head, grabs my hand, and pulls it to his private parts. It's hard in my hand, just like the last time he made me touch him.

"Is this what happens when people kiss?"

"Not everyone."

"Then why is it happening to you?"

"Because my cock wants inside you, Little Nun. I want to defile you in ways that would make your God cringe." I instantly jerk my hand away from him and step back, although he never moves. He stares at me with those dark pits he calls eyes, and all I can do is stare back at them.

"Why do you want me?"

"I don't know, Ash. You're nothing like what I'm into."

"I don't understand."

"I don't go for the good girls, Ash. I want a bad girl. I want a girl who will take my cock and use it like it's meant to be used."

"Like the girl the other night?" I'm almost embarrassed to bring that up again.

"No. Not like her. She's a whore I used to get off, and nothing more, but you? You're becoming something I'm obsessed with, and that's a bad thing, Little Nun."

"I want to know more about you." I blurt the words out, although I don't know why. I shouldn't have said that. I shouldn't want to know more about him, but I do.

"No."

"Why?"

"You're not ready for that part of me. You're too pure," he tells me.

"Then make me dirty." His eyes burn straight through me as I look at him. I can feel the heat between us, and I think he knows there's something here, too. I don't want to admit it because that would be admitting I'm a sinner, and I don't want to be that, but I also can't keep living a life I'm not sure I want.

Before I can speak again, Tristan has my face in his hands, devouring my lips with his. He kisses me in ways I've never been kissed before, and when his tongue slides into my mouth, I moan for him.

My body tingles, and heat runs wild inside me from the way he's kissing me. Then he pulls back and shakes his head, tugging at his hair.

"You're making a big fucking mistake, Ash."

"I don't think I am."

"Yeah, you are. Now stay the hell away from me." It's a warning I doubt I'm going to take. I don't want to stay away from him. I want to get closer and closer to him.

Chapter 9
Tristan

I let Ash come to the warehouse to watch me sculpt today. I don't know why. The model isn't here today, but I have plenty in my mind to work with.

"You make it all by hand? Even if it's that big?" she asks as I keep working.

"All by hand."

"What else can you sculpt?"

"Just about anything you want."

"What about me?" Now my eyes jerk over to where she sits on a stool watching me.

"Why would I?"

"Because I asked you to."

"Naked? You're comfortable getting naked in front of me?" She shakes her head, and I laugh. "I didn't think so. Shut up and sit there being a good Little Nun." I get back to work and ignore her for the most part, but that fucking electricity that runs between us is almost too much for me to deal with without fucking her senseless. I know she wants it. I can see the look in her eyes, but I'm not about to give it to her yet.

"Will you be naked?" She finally asks.

"You want me to be?" I ask in return.

"I'd feel more comfortable, I think," she answers, chewing on her nail.

"What if I just make you a cute little cross? How about that?"

"I mean it. I want to try, Tristan." I swallow hard because seeing her naked is only going to fuck with my head more, and I know it. But I nod my fucking head and motion for her to strip. I step back and take off all my clothes, standing in front of her naked. Her eyes roam over my body, and it hits me that she's never seen a man naked before. She stops on my cock, and that bastard jerks at her attention.

"I don't know what to say."

"Don't say anything. Take it off," I order, nodding toward the dress she has on today. She slowly pulls it over her head and drops it to the floor. "All of it." She moves to her bra, then her panties, and a fucking growl lodges in my throat. Seeing her naked is just solidifying the fact I should stay as far from her as possible.

"This is a bad idea," I tell her once more.

"Please." That one word coming from her lips is all I can handle. I step toward her slowly and then once again. She watches me, unsure what I'm about to do. I reach for her hair, wrapping it around my hand to pull her head back so she's forced to look at me. Her lips part as she keeps her eyes on mine.

"You're asking a lot of me when I have little restraint."

"I'm not your type. You said so yourself," she reminds me of my own words.

"Your body is."

"That doesn't make sense."

"It doesn't need to. We're human. We're feral. We do what we need for pleasure."

Ash swallows hard before reaching up and untangling my hand from her hair. Then she walks over to the stool and takes a seat, crossing her legs. I go back to what I was supposed to do and begin to sculpt her on a smaller scale than my other works.

Ash watches me, and the fire in her eyes is almost more than I can deal with right now. I want to take her, break her, fuck her, hurt her. There are so many things I want to do to her that I know she'll regret later.

So I focus. I focus on the sculpture, on making it look just like her.

Ash sits for hours, my cock eventually calming himself down as I work.

"It has to dry," I tell her when I'm finished and move past her.

"Can I look at it?"

"Yeah." She stands from the stool and walks over, looking at it with a smile and awe on her face.

"This is amazing."

"It's you."

"Meaning what?"

"Meaning nothing. I'm taking a shower." I leave her standing there looking at her sculpture and head into the bathroom, starting the water. A few seconds later, the door opens, and she enters the bathroom.

"What the fuck are you doing?"

"Coming to shower with you."

"You're being awfully brave for a Little Nun."

"You told me to ask. That's it. And I want to know what you feel like," she says, her voice hitching when she speaks.

"Inside you?" She shakes her head. "Under your palms? Against your skin?" Now, she slowly nods her head, and I nod mine, too. I started this shit with her. I let her think she can do what she wants with me as long as she asks me. "Fine."

She steps into the large shower, and I do the same. The water hits me, and I wash the clay off me when I feel her hands on my back. I stop moving. I stiffen at her touch because this, this is far more than crossing the line. This is taking a full fucking leap over the goddamn edge of my sanity.

Her hands roam over my back. Every fucking muscle in my body is locked up tightly, with her touching me. I want to tell her to stop. I want to beg her to keep going, but I do neither. I stand as still as I can and let her touch me.

When I turn to face her, she looks down and I know what she wants.

"Little Unholy one, aren't you?"

"Can I?"

"Ash," I warn her.

"Just one touch." Fuck. She's trying to kill me. That's what this is. It's mental fucking warfare, and she's winning. I nod my head and close my eyes so I don't have to look her in the eyes as she does it because I know if I do, I'll lose it and take her against her will right here, right now. And maybe that's what she wants. She wants me to fuck her against the wall of my shower.

I think about doing it when her hand rests on my cock. Again, that fucker jerks to life for her. She slowly begins to move her hand over it, fingering the vein underneath as I groan.

"Ash, this isn't going to work."

"I just want to see what it feels like," she whispers as she keeps her hand moving. Finally, she wraps it around and begins to stroke it the way I made her stroke it the last time I had her touch my cock. I bite my fucking lip until I taste blood because her hand feels too damn good wrapped around me like this. I start to roll my hips into her hand, getting into a good rhythm. It all feels so fucking good that I reach for her, dragging her face to mine and devouring her mouth. My blood leaks onto her tongue, and she moans the more I kiss her, but her little hand doesn't stop moving until I'm coming all over her. Cum hits her stomach and slowly slides down her flesh when I release her with one hand and slip it down her stomach. I collect the cum and find her clit, rubbing it until her knees begin to shake.

"What's that?"

"You're going to come for me, Ash. That's all it is. A fucking orgasm like you never felt before," I tell her. I play with her clit, getting her worked up before I slow down and start all over. I keep going, using my cum as lube and wrapping my other arm around her to hold her up because when she comes, she fucking explodes.

"Tristan!" My name leaves her mouth in a fucking scream that I wish her little boyfriend could hear. Her body convulses and shivers as I keep pressure on her clit.

When her eyes begin to roll back, I ease up on her as she tries so hard to catch her breath.

"Nobody has ever touched me there," she says softly.

"And you just let your stepbrother, the most sinister thing you can see, touch you. How does it feel?" I ask her wondering what she will say.

"I don't even know. I've never felt anything like that."

"You want more?"

"Can I have more?" I chuckle now.

"You can have whatever you want, Ash. I told you, just ask."

Chapter 10
Ash

I don't know how I feel. I let him touch me. I touched him. This is wrong. It's all so wrong, and yet I wanted more. I wanted to see what he felt like inside me, but I didn't ask him. I was too afraid of what that might mean to the two of us.

"You ready?" Amy asks as I fix my dress and my hair.

"Are you, is the better question?" She laughs at me and then pulls me into a side hug.

"I love your dad. He's a wonderful man. And thank you for giving Tristan a chance. I know he's different," she says.

"He's really not that bad." Now she tenses.

"I didn't say that, Ash. Tristan has more demons than any of us realize. The things he likes and does, I don't even want to know all of it."

"He doesn't seem that bad."

"He's not when he's under control. It's when he loses that control," she admits to me. I nod my head.

"I'll be careful around him."

"Good. I don't want you getting hurt," she adds. I nod my head, and the music begins to play. We step out of the room and Tristan is there waiting. He hugs his mom and tells her she's beautiful before offering me his arm. I slide mine through his, and we begin to walk toward the door.

"You've been avoiding me," he says as we walk.

"It's for the best."

"Why is that?"

"I have a boyfriend, and I allowed you to touch me. It's a sin."

"I think we're way past the sinning stage, don't you?" he asks. I look up at him and shake my head.

"I've realized I should have stopped myself and I didn't. That's my sin to carry."

"Stop with this sinning shit, Ash. We were both there. You wanted it," he tells me.

"And now I don't."

"I bet you're fucking wet for me right now. How are you going to walk down the aisle on my arm with that slickness between your thighs?" Shivers roll over my body, and he can see it. Bumps form on my flesh from his words, and I have to take a deep breath to calm myself down.

"Could you not talk like that right now, please?"

"Later then?"

"Tristan," I say when the doors open, and it's our turn to walk down the aisle. Tristan keeps me close to him, a little too close if you ask me, as we make our way down to the front. Once we're there, we move off to our sides, and that's where we stand. When the doors open again, it's his mom walking out.

She looks beautiful in her long gown, but it makes me wonder if my dad treats her the same way as he does me. A sadness forms inside me at the thought of her having to live that way for the rest of her life. The way my mom lived that way until she died.

A single tear falls down my cheek, and I quickly wipe it away. Tristan watches his mom as she walks closer to us. Then, when she's right in front of us, and my dad takes his place, his eyes come back to me. It makes me squirm, knowing he's watching me the way he is.

The ceremony continues, and they vow to love each other for the rest of their days. I can't wait for this to be over because I'd like to ask Tristan about his mom. I know a little about her, but not a lot. Like will she put up with my dad's idea of punishment?

We make it to the reception and that's when Tristan and I are forced to dance together. Ben would be so upset if he saw us like this because, oddly enough, I find I like being in Tristan's arms.

We dance all night and he even says sweet things that make me smile and laugh. I wasn't sure Tristan had this side to him, but I can see it now.

He twirls me around and pulls me back into his arms before leaning down and whispering in my ear.

"I want to make you come all over my tongue."

"What?"

"You heard me. I want to taste you, Ash."

"No. I … I can't do that."

"Why not? I've had my hands on you."

"That's different, and I've already punished myself for that."

"What did you do?"

"I poured my soul out to God and begged for forgiveness. I prayed while I was kneeling on the broomstick."

"You hurt yourself like he does?" he growls low in his throat.

"It's punishment for my sins, Tristan. I'm sorry, but this is done," I tell him. I can't do this. I can't be what he wants me to be.

"You'll regret saying those words."

"No, I won't. Ben and I are going to get married and raise a family. I need to focus on that and school."

"So, you think I'm shit like everyone else does?" he asks. Why does he have to say it like that? I don't think of him that way.

"No, you're not. But you are my brother now."

73

"Fuck that. How many brothers do you know made their sister come with his cum? How many brothers know what his sister feels like?" My cheeks burn like fire when he says it. I remember every single second of it and how it felt, how he felt.

"It's over now, Tristan. I'm sorry."

"You know what? Fuck you, Ash. Fuck you, and fuck this family bullshit. I want no part of your little bible-thumping world. When you're ready to bow to your real God, you find me." With that he pulls himself away from me and walks off. I follow behind him because this is wrong. He shouldn't be acting like this.

"Tristan, wait."

"You want me, Little Nun?" he asks when he turns to face me.

"You know we can't be like that."

"Why not? Because your little fairytale of God and Heaven won't allow it? Well, guess what? It's all bullshit, Ash. All of it!"

"I'm so sorry," I tell him. He laughs darkly and shakes his head.

"No. You're not, but you will be." I watch him walk out of the reception, pulling a cigarette out as he goes. I sigh and go back to the party talking with some of the other guests. That is until we hear tires squealing and metal crunching.

In my heart, I know it's him. In my head, I pray it isn't.

We rush out the side door to see his car wrapped around a telephone pole.

"Tristan!" His mom yells as we rush toward the scene. People are on their phones calling for help, and all I can feel is panic. What if he didn't make it? What if this is all my fault? No. I can't think like that. He's okay. He has to be.

"Ash!" My dad calls to me, and I turn to look at him as he pulls a bloody Tristan from the car. "Come help!" I've had some training in first aid but not trauma training. Not for this.

I rush toward them and start doing the best I can for him when someone else yells.

"Get back! The car is going to explode!" Everyone moves except me. I can't leave him here. I won't do that. I lift under his arms and pull him toward safety while his mom watches in shock, and my dad does nothing to help. Not that it surprises me. He doesn't like Tristan, and his mom is too stunned to move.

"Help me!" I scream at anyone who will listen to me. Someone rushes from the crowd and helps me pull him to safety right before the car goes up in flames. I fall on my butt, his head landing in my lap. I move to shift him off me and lay him on the ground so I can get back to work. I rip the bottom of my dress and press it against his wounds, trying to stop the bleeding until help arrives.

I don't know what I'm thinking or feeling right now. There's too much happening, too much going on. He's bleeding a lot, and I don't have enough hands to keep the bleeding under control. I yell for more help, but my voice is scratchy, and people I don't recognize move in to help me.

Is this my fault?

Chapter 11
Tristan

I groan as I turn my head to see my mom sitting in the chair next to me. Fuck, I'm still alive. That wasn't exactly the plan. The plan was to make the Little Nun of mine feel something she'd never felt before. Fear of loss. Fear of losing me. Not that I belong to her to lose, but the thought of her crying for me does something to my insides. I guess that shit backfired on me, though, since I'm still here, and she isn't.

"Mom?"

"Tristan. Oh, you're awake," she cries while tears stream down her face.

"I'm okay."

"No, you're not. You're hurt. You had surgery. What happened?"

"I don't know. I just lost control of the car," I lie to her. I'm not going to tell her I slammed into the fucking pole to get Ash's attention. Not a chance in hell.

"I'm so glad you're awake. You didn't damage anything major, but they did have to do surgery to repair some things. You're lucky, Tristan." I nod my head as I look at her still in her wedding dress and know that I fucked up her day. That wasn't the plan. This was all for Ash, and that was a complete fuck up.

"Go home."

"What? No."

"Yeah. It's your wedding day. Go on your honeymoon. I'm fine."

"No, Tristan."

"I said to go!" I yell this time, shocking her, but I don't know why. She knows this about me. I'm a bastard. A monster.

"Fine. Your therapist will be in to see you tomorrow." I nod my head and watch her stand and leave. It doesn't take long before Andy and Rod show up to see me.

"Glad you're not dead."

"I'm not."

"What the hell, man?" Rod asks.

"This life sucks," I laugh a little. They both shake their heads and smile, knowing me better than most people do.

"Just glad you're okay. Doc said we can't stay we could only drop in," Andy tells me.

"Fuck that doctor."

"You look like shit, so that's good news," Rod tells me with a laugh. They both turn to leave when Andy steps back.

"Your stepsister has been pacing all night. You want her in here?"

"No."

"Okay. Get some rest. We'll check on you tomorrow." I nod and salute the two of them when they walk out. Seconds later, she was in my room after I said no.

"I don't want you here," I tell her.

"Are you insane? No. Don't answer that. You are insane, Tristan! What were you thinking? Why would you do that?"

"You don't know what I did," I tell her. Seeing her still wearing the bloody dress does something to me. I want her. More than I've ever wanted anyone in my life, but I'll bring her even more hurt than I see on her face right now, and maybe that's the sick part of me. Maybe that's what the darkest part of me wants. Her hurt. Her pain.

"You slammed into a pole!"

"Get out."

"No. A pole, Tristan," she snaps at me.

"I said get out."

"I'm not leaving you like this."

"You said you didn't want me, Ash. Get the fuck out!" I roar this time. She crosses her arms over her chest and stomps over, sitting in the chair next to the bed. If I could get up, I would probably snap her pretty little neck right now or sink my teeth into her soft flesh.

"They think you did this on purpose."

"And if I did?"

"Why would you? Did you want to die? Is that it?"

"What difference does it make to you?"

"Tristan, come on. Don't be like that."

"Like what? Telling you the truth? You want the truth? Yeah, I slammed that car into the pole on purpose. Now get out!" Just as the words come out of my mouth, the fucking doc walks in.

"Suicide attempt, Tristan?" Fuck me.

"Doc, you came."

"They called and told me what happened. You know what that means?" he says.

"What does it mean?" Ash asks before I can respond.

"It means, fuck you, Ash."

"It means he stays on a seventy-two hour hold until we know he isn't a danger to himself anymore."

"What?" Ash asks.

"What happened to patient-doctor confidentiality?" I ask him.

"This her?" Doc asks me, and I nod.

"I'm Arnold, his Doctor. I have been his doctor since he was three," he tells her. She looks at me and back to him before finally shaking his hand.

"It's nice to meet you, Dr."

"Arnold is fine. You're going to have to leave so we can get his treatment started."

"What treatment?"

"I have to be med-compliant in order to get out after seventy-two hours," I inform her.

"Medication? You don't take any." She adds as if she already knows all about me. That's so fucking cute it makes me want to throw up.

"Just get out, Ash. This isn't your problem."

"You made it my problem, Tristan."

"No. You're making it your problem. I said what I needed to say to you. What fucking part of leave don't you get?" I turn my head so she can see the look on my face and it isn't a nice one.

"Fine. I'll see you when you get home."

"If I make it home," I tell her.

"Don't say that."

"I just did. Bye, Ash." I turn away from her, needing her out of my fucking face before I do something else stupid for her. Just for her to fucking see me? What kind of fuck up am I?

Doc leads her out, but I can still hear them in the hallway. He's just giving her a breakdown of what's going to happen and when I can go home. He's not responding to her questions. He can't. That's confidential.

When he's done, he comes back into the room and sits in the chair that Ash was in.

"She seems nice."

I snort a laugh. "Yeah. Nice."

"What do you see in her, Tristan?"

"What's the difference?"

"She said she didn't want you, right? Is that what this is about? We've talked about rejection, haven't we?"

"Yeah, Doc, we have."

"Then what is it with her?" he pushes, trying to pry into my fucked up mind.

"You know what? I felt numb. Felt nothing. So I slammed into that fucking pole so I'd feel something, and I did," I chuckle.

"Take the medicine, Tristan."

"You don't even know what the fuck you're treating me for!" I remind him.

"It doesn't matter at this point. I think they'll help," he tells me.

"Like the last ones? When I was a fucking zombie? That's what you want for me?"

"I want you stable, Tristan. I don't want you out there slamming into poles to feel something."

"You know when I felt something? When she was in my shower."

"You didn't sleep with her, did you?" I shake my head.

"No."

"You need to step back and stay away from her, Tristan. This isn't healthy."

"Hey, Doc? Fuck off, man. I don't need you telling me shit I already know. Lock me the fuck up on the fifth floor, and let's get this over with." I ignore the rest of the shit that leaves his mouth because, frankly, Fuck him.

After the other Doc gives his approval, I'm moved to the psych ward. It's not like I haven't been here more than once. I'm put into a room, and my fucking arms and legs are strapped down so I can't try and kill myself again. My stomach hurts where they performed the surgery, but I welcome the fucking pain.

I close my eyes and try to keep from thinking about the girl. Thinking about the way she looked at me and how she yelled at me. I can't be with her. The Doc is right. This is going to kill me, and while I'm not opposed to going straight to hell, I know my mom would lose it. Not that it should bother me. I've never cared much before, but I do love my mom.

I tip my head back and try to sleep, but hearing people screaming and groaning all fucking night does little more than drive me a little further into my head. If they think for one fucking second keeping me locked up in this hell hole is helping me, they're dead wrong. All it's doing is making me feel worse.

Chapter 12
Ash

Dad and Amy went on their honeymoon in Spain. I'm happy for them and today Tristan comes home. I informed his Doctor I would be the one picking him up, and they said that was fine since he's an adult.

I step into the basement to get his things in order when I see the painting on the easel. Is that? That can't be me. I walk over and run my fingers over the angel he's painted with my face. I swallow hard as I take it in. It's beautiful. I've never seen anything as beautiful as this. Knowing he wouldn't want me to see it, I flip it around so the back is facing out. Then I finish picking up his room before heading out to pick him up.

I'm ushered into a waiting area when I arrive. When they wheel him out, I'm confused. He's not alert. He's in a wheelchair, not even walking.

"What's wrong with him?"

"He's on a lot of medication right now. It'll wear off. Here's his prescriptions," the woman says, handing a bagful of bottles. I look at them and then back at her like she's insane. That's a lot of meds for one person.

"He needs to follow up with his regular doctor in three days," she explains. I nod my head before I step behind him and push his near lifeless body out of the room and into the elevator.

"Tristan?" I call his name, but he doesn't respond and I can understand why. He has to be overmedicated. I shake my head, push him out when the doors open, and go out to my car. I help him into the front seat before returning the chair and coming back. His head rests against the window, and his eyes are closed.

I get in and start the car, driving us back to the house. When we arrive, I help him out and inside.

"Do you want to stay on the couch?" I ask him, not knowing if he's going to make it down the steps. He shakes his head, and I do the best I can to help him walk down the stairs without both of us falling. I'm basically dragging him to his bed and helping him lay down before pulling the blankets over him. When I start to pull away, he grabs my wrist and whispers.

"Stay."

"That's not a good idea," I tell him.

"Please." With that one word, that's all it took. Just hearing him say please in that sad tone has broken me. I nod my head even if he can't see me and crawl onto the bed next to him. I know he did what he did because of me, and I shouldn't be here, but how can I not be here?

His hand finds mine and he intertwines our fingers, holding on as tightly as he can. I'm not sure what to do now. I try to sleep, listening to him snore lightly next to me. I know the medication has to be taking a toll on his body, as well as the surgery he had.

I finally doze off and when I wake up, he's staring at me. I gasp and start to shift away, but his hand lands on my hip, keeping me in place. Neither of us speaks as he moves in closer, pressing his lips to mine. I let him kiss me and start to kiss him back. This is wrong. I can feel it in every single bone in my body. I shouldn't be here, in his bed, kissing him. But why does it feel so right then? Why doesn't this feel wrong?

When he stops kissing me, and his hand begins to move over me, I pull away.

"Be with me, Ash." His words send heat coiling inside me, but I shake my head no.

"I can't do that."

"Do you have any idea how much I fucking need you, Ash? How much it hurts when you walk away from me?" Tears immediately fill my eyes as I shake my head.

"Don't say that."

"It's true. It's like you're ripping my fucking black heart out," he adds. I think it's just the medicine talking, but he looks like himself this morning.

"I can't be what you need," I tell him.

"You don't know what I need."

"I can't be like her. I'm not her."

"I don't want her, Ash. Be with me."

"What about Ben?" I ask him.

"Fuck Ben. He doesn't need you the way I do," he tells me. My heart leaps in my chest a little at his words. I don't know what to say. Do I feel a connection to Tristan? Yeah, I do, but we're so different this could never work out between us.

"I can't."

"Don't walk away from me, Ash. I won't live to see another day if you do." It's a threat. I can hear it in his tone.

"No. You don't get to do that! You don't get to threaten me, Tristan."

"I'm not threatening. Just … fuck. Get out," he orders, looking the other way. It hurts. I felt an ache deep inside my chest when he turned his head and looked the other way.

Do I want to be with Tristan? Part of me says yes, but the other part, the more rational part, says to run the other way because I can't and never will be what he needs. However, what if he's telling the truth? What if he does need me?

Going against my better judgment, I reach for him, grabbing his face in my hand and turning it back to face me.

"I don't know what I'm doing, Tristan. It feels wrong and right at the same time," I tell him truthfully.

"Nothing right is ever wrong, Ash." He leans in, pressing his lips to mine once more, and I find myself savoring every bit of him. His hand stays on my hip for a short time before he pulls away and pushes me onto my back. Then, his hand slides into the top of my jeans. The ones I wore, knowing he'd see me in them.

"You wore the jeans," he makes a note.

"I'm finding I like them."

"Me too," he whispers as his hand sinks into the front of my panties. I suck in a rigid breath when he slowly dips a finger inside me.

"So fucking tight," he says as he works a finger in a little more. I've never felt anything like this. Nothing at all, and I know I should be ashamed, but I'm not. It feels too good to even think about feeling that way.

"I want to fuck you, Little Nun. I want to dirty you up with my body." His words have my breathing picking up speed, and I don't know how to stop it from happening. He works his finger in and out of me, and I whine. He keeps going, hitting a spot inside that nearly has me leaping off the bed.

"Tell me. Tell me I can fuck you, Ash."

"I don't know. We're not married," I tell him because that's the way it should be, right? We should be married before sex.

"That's so old school. You know that, right? Hell, mom was probably fucking your dad before they got married," he replies casually.

"Isn't it personal? I mean, shouldn't it mean something?"

"You think it won't mean anything? It'll mean you're mine, Ash. Some people believe when you kiss you belong to that person. I believe when I sunk my teeth into your flesh, you became mine."

"I can't … we can't …"

"We can. Just say the words, and I'm going to bury my fucking secrets inside you."

I lie in his bed while he slides his finger in and out of me in the most delicious ways I've ever felt, and I'm torn. Do I do this? It goes against everything I've ever learned. No sex before marriage, but I let him touch me, and I shouldn't have done that either.

"Okay."

"Yeah?" he asks. I nod my head, and he leans over, kissing me once more. I can tell he's still in pain, but that doesn't stop him from getting to work on our clothes. He winces when he pulls his off, and I offer him his pain meds.

"They make me tired, and I don't want to fucking sleep, Ash. I want inside you like I've never wanted anything before."

Once he has us both naked, he grabs the condom from his table and slides it on. His penis seems bigger than the last time I saw it, and that scares me a little.

"Will it fit?"

"Aww, Little Nun. Your pussy is made to stretch. There's no way in fuck I'm not getting it inside you."

"You had surgery," I remind him.

"And it hurts like fuck, but I need this more than the pain meds. I don't think you get it. I thrive on the fucking pain, Ash. Give me all the pain." I nod my head as Tristan spreads my legs and climbs in between them. I don't know what to do so I just lie here.

Chapter 13
Tristan

Insane. That's what I feel looking down at her fucking wet pussy waiting for me. Crazy. Worse than I'd ever felt before. And it's all because of her. I'm insane, and I blame her for partly. After this, after I'm inside her, I know that I'm never going to be the same, and I'm kissing her neck, debating whether I should do it.

The Doc would say no. Stay the hell away from that girl but how the hell can I?

"Will it hurt?"

"I'm bigger than most guys, Ash. It's going to hurt, and sadly, I'm going to love every second of hurting you."

"Why?"

"Because it's what I do. I thrive on pain. Mine or others." She nods her head as I grab my cock and position it at her entrance. I debate going slow, letting her adjust, or just fucking her hard. Both options war in my head, but only one wins.

I thrust roughly into her, and she screams for me. Her hands come up, her nails digging into my back, and I savor every second of the burn as she breaks my skin.

"That's it, Ash. Fucking mark me," I growl as I pull back just to drive into her once again. I keep going, needing her like I've never needed anything in my life. I don't know if it's just a phase, but something in my head says it's not.

It says that this is more, that I fucking need her more than I would if it was just a phase.

I roll my hips, fucking her long and hard, and she keeps crying out for more. My Little Nun is now tainted and defiled because of me. Not that she wasn't already because I did do other things to her but this? This just solidifies what I've been wanting to do to her.

My hips buck, fucking her like I'm a starved man, and for her, I am. This is everything I thought it would be and more.

"Fuck, Ash. This is too good," I growl as I keep going. There's no stopping me right now, but then her phone rings. I glance over as I slow down and see it's Ben and smirk.

"Answer it," I tell her. She shakes her head. "I said, answer it." It's an order this time. I grab the phone and pass it to her, keeping a slow pace as she presses the button.

"Hello?" I keep fucking her while she's on the phone with her soon to be ex boyfriend. I keep going because there's no way I can stop myself now that I'm inside her. I lean down and bite her shoulder once more, marking me as my own.

"I'm … I'm fine." I hear the one-sided conversation before I start to pick up my pace. Ash can't handle it and hangs up the phone. Ben calls right back, but her hands are gripping my forearms as I take her faster.

"You're a bad Little Nun. You know that? You like having my cock deep inside of you, don't you? You like the feel of me in you. How'd you like talking to your ex while I'm ruining this pussy?" She's gasping for air, moaning like crazy, and I still can't get enough.

A few more rough thrusts into her, and I feel her body tense.

"Tristan!" She calls out for me.

"You're going to come, baby. That's it. Keep fucking doing that," I tell her until her whole body begins to tremble and she releases. I follow behind her, coming like a crazed man inside her. My cock jerks, releasing everything that's been pent up inside me from being around her.

When I'm done, I pull out and drop next to her.

"Am I bleeding?" she asks, looking down at my condom-covered cock. I glance down and grin.

"Yeah, you are. For me, Ash. You're fucking bleeding for me."

"I need to clean this up."

"No. Leave it alone. We'll shower later."

"Isn't that gross?"

"No. It's not. It's sexy as fuck I made you bleed like that. I was the first one inside you, Ash, and I'm going to be the last." She sighs, and I reach for her, pulling her into me. She rests her head on my chest, careful not to touch my stomach, but I want the pain. I crave it.

"How do you feel?"

"Tired," she yawns. I chuckle a little.

"Try to sleep. We'll grab dinner later," I tell her. She nods her head, and her warm breath dances over my flesh as she finally falls asleep. I lie still, letting her sleep as I think about what I've just done. I've ruined her purity. I've taken something she held so dearly to her, and I don't even feel bad. In the back of my mind, I think I should, but I don't. She's mine. I knew it the first time I laid eyes on her that she was going to be mine. I just had to figure out how to make that happen.

When Ash wakes up back, we shower and I clean her up before we head out to grab something to eat.

"Can I ask you something?" she asks.

"Yeah."

"The crash. You did it on purpose, Tristan."

"So?"

"So, is this something I have to worry about all the time? You doing something crazy?" I lean my elbows on the table in front of me and look directly into her eyes.

"I'm not normal, Ash. Never will be, and sometimes I do stupid shit that doesn't seem so stupid at the time."

"Why did you do it?"

"You told me you were staying away from me. I couldn't have that."

"You did it so I wouldn't walk away?"

"Partially. The other part, I did it because I wanted to fucking feel something again."

"I can't be with you if you keep doing those things," she tells me.

"I can't promise what I will and won't do. It's not how my brain works, Ash."

"Will you try at least?" I nod my head.

"I can do that much."

"Okay. As long as you try."

"Then you're willing to be with me?" I ask her, needing to hear her fucking say the words. I need to hear it come out of her mouth, yet it doesn't really matter to me. She's mine now, even if I have to kill Ben for getting in my way. I'm not letting her go.

"I'll be with you."

"And Ben?"

"I don't know what to say about Ben. I need to break it to him gently," she says.

"He's not a baby."

"Compared to you, he is."

"What does that mean?"

"I'm just saying he doesn't have a hardened exterior like you do. He's breakable," she explains as I chuckle.

"Whatever you say. As long as he doesn't put his hands on you, I'm fine with it."

"He won't."

"Good. Because I'd have no problem killing him," I add. Her eyes widen before she sees the look in mine. She has to know I'd do it. I'd fucking cut his insides out and shove them back down his throat.

"Do you have work to do?" she asks, changing the subject.

"A little. Why?"

"Can I come?" Now I smile.

"You can come anytime, Ash. You don't need to ask."

"Will there be other girls there?" I shake my head.

"No. Just you."

"Okay." We finish our food and then head over to the warehouse, where I get back to work on the sculptures. Ash sits off to the side on the sofa, watching me so intently, like she has nothing better to do. Her eyes stay glued to everything I'm doing, and I couldn't fucking be happier than I am right now.

One would think after the surgery that I shouldn't be doing this, but no one understands the way I need the pain to feel something, anything. I love the feeling, the ache.

Chapter 14
Ash

It's insane the way that man can work with his hands. The amount of detail he puts into his work. His mom must be really proud of him for all that he's accomplished.

Me, on the other hand? I haven't done anything. I didn't even go to the youth center like I had planned. I've been too wrapped up in Tristan, and maybe that's wrong.

"Will you take me out?" I ask him, catching his attention.

"Where?"

"Wherever you go. I want to see what it's like being you," I tell him. I've been wondering what it would be like to hang out at the places Tristan does.

"I don't think that's a good idea."

"Why not?"

"Because you're not like me, Ash."

"And that's supposed to mean what?" I huff now. I can handle myself with him, so I should be fine with his friends.

"You know what? Never mind. I'll take you," he says, getting back to work. I grin because I finally have a win with him. He's going to take me out and show me what he likes to do with his free time. Not that I would know what I like to do. I haven't done anything.

I watch as he finishes what he's working on and then cleans himself up. He comes back out of the bathroom with wet hair and black clothes as per his usual. He walks over, pulls me off the chair, and spins me around, making me laugh before he pulls me into him.

"We're going to do so many things together," he tells me.

"Like what?"

"I can't ruin the surprise for you, Little Nun, but when I get done with you, you're going to be the Little Unholy." My heart leaps inside of me a little, and I don't know if it's from fear or excitement. Or maybe a little of both.

"Is this wrong?"

"Nothing is wrong," he says before pulling me by my hand and out of the warehouse.

"Why do you have so many snakes?"

"I have two. A boa named Max and a python named Jones."

"They're big," I tell him as we climb on his bike, and he passes me a helmet.

"They're not fully grown yet. They're basically babies."

"That's a baby?" I ask, not sure I heard him right. There's no way. Those things are huge.

"Yeah."

"Aren't they dangerous?"

"If not handled correctly, they are, but I know what I'm doing."

I shrug as he tugs my arms around him and then revs his bike. We take off down the road, and I smile behind the helmet. I love this. I know it's only the second time I've been on his bike, but this is perfect.

He stops the bike at the same place I hid in his trunk. When the helmet is off, Tristan grabs my hand and leads me down the steps and inside the place once again. This time, he crosses the room with me in tow and drops down into the chair, pulling me into his lap.

"Well, look who decided to come see us," one of the guys sitting there says as he eyes me and Tristan.

"You miss me, fuckers?" Tristan asks.

"Thought you were locked up," the other says.

"They released me after seventy-two hours."

"I take it you're not on the meds?" Tristan shakes his head as if they should have already known that and then orders a few beers and a shot. I watch him take down the shot and then the beer like it's nothing before he offers it to me. I shake my head. I'm not a drinker and never have been.

"You wanted to see what it was like," he tells me. He goes on and introduces me to his friends as I sip on the beer, even though it's nasty.

"So you're the stepsister, huh?" Andy asks.

"That's me."

"He said you were a bible thumper," Rod inserts himself into the conversation now.

"I am. I was. I honestly don't know what I am anymore," I admit to them.

"Nothing wrong with that. Fuck, we don't know who we are most days. The thing is, you should never let anyone tell you what or who you should be, right? You're your own person. There shouldn't be any fucking judgment from anyone." He's right. I shouldn't be judged for who I want to be, but I don't know who that is anymore.

Tristan has shown me a side of myself I didn't know I had, and now I want to explore that more. But if my dad finds out, he'll surely lock me away so I can never see Tristan again.

"I'm just enjoying feeling free. I don't think I've felt that in a long time," I tell them. Tristan's hand clamps down on my thigh, giving it a little squeeze when another girl comes walking over.

"What's this?"

"What's what?" Andy asks her.

"Who the hell is she?"

"She's my girl," Tristan tells her. I can see the anger in her gaze and by the way she looks at me, she isn't happy I'm here.

"Since when?"

"Since I fucked her senseless, that's when." I tense a little, not knowing he was going to tell her that, but then again, Tristan isn't one to hold back.

"Was that before or after I sucked you off?" she asks. Now, I move off Tristan's lap and rush toward the stairs as quickly as I can.

I hear him laughing behind me, but when I rush up the steps, he's already there, wrapping his arm around my waist and dragging me back into him.

"Let me go."

"You wanted this, Little Nun."

"I didn't need to hear about all the girls you slept with."

"Did you think it was only you?"

"I … I don't know what I thought!"

"I've fucked other people, Ash. I don't plan on it while I'm with you," he tells me. I slowly relax into his hold and he spins me in his arms so I'm facing him.

"I can't do what she did."

"What?"

"Suck you or whatever she's talking about." Now, he laughs once more.

"Oh, you can, and you will. She's just being a bitch to try and piss you off. Why are you letting her?"

"What? Because I'm here with you and clearly she has an issue with that!" I snap at him.

"You think I give a shit about her issue? No, I damn well don't, and neither should you. You wanted to know what it's like to be me? Then try not giving a shit, Ash. Fuck her."

"You did," I remind him. He laughs again, and this time, I find myself smiling with him.

"See that? You did good just now. Fuck her, Ash. Really, she means nothing." I nod my head, and he leads me back down the stairs and back inside, where his friends are still drinking.

"Don't let that bitch get to you, Ash. She's fucked half this club," Andy informs me. That doesn't really make me feel any better, but now I'm kind of glad it wasn't just Tristan.

"Already forgotten," I tell them as they pass me another drink. I sip on this one until my head gets a little fuzzy and listen to the guys talking and just messing around.

My body feels hot, too hot. My insides are burning as Tristan runs his hand up and down my thigh. I gasp when he moves it slightly higher.

"Tristan," I whisper his name near his ear.

"Yeah?"

"I feel warm and tingly all over." He laughs and presses a kiss to the side of my head.

"It's the alcohol," he tells me. "It'll make you feel like that."

"No. It's like I need something," I admit to him.

"You're horny, Little Nun?" he asks me. I don't know what that feels like, but if this is it, then yes.

"I don't know," I tell him. He leans in, nipping my earlobe, sending more heat coursing through my body.

"I need you, Tristan," I tell him.

"You have me."

"You know what I mean. I think … I think I need sex," I whisper causing him to laugh once more. He bites my earlobe harder this time and nods his head.

"Home or here?"

"Home?" I ask him. He nods his head, but then I see some strange look in his eyes. He moves his gaze from me to someone else and then to his friends. They both see what I don't.

"What?" I ask. Tristan shoves me off his lap before standing and moving toward some other guy. His fist pulls back and slams into his face before I hear the name Shane leave his mouth. The man falls to the floor with Tristan on top of him, but I'm so out of it right now that I don't know what to do but stand and watch.

His friends move in to pull him away from the guy's lifeless body, and that's when he turns to me and grins. I should be scared, but with this much alcohol in me, I'm not.

"Fuck, Tristan," one of the guys says, but I can't tell who. The room is spinning, and my body is humming with need. Need for Tristan.

"You see that, Little Nun? That's who the fuck I am!" Tristan yells as his friends usher us toward the steps.

"Go home. We'll handle this," Andy says as he shoves us toward the steps. Tristan grabs my hand with his bloody one and drags me up the stairs and toward the bike quickly. He shoves the helmet on my head and forces me onto the bike before he's on it, and we're taking off.

Chapter 15
Tristan

She's naked on my bed, writhing with need as I tease her with my fingers that as still covered in Shane's blood. She arches into me, needing me inside her, and I plan on giving that to her after I'm done toying with her.

I glance over at Max, and a new idea hits me. I leave Ash lying there and walk over, taking him from his tank as she watches me with a confused look on her face.

"What are you doing?" she asks the closer I get to her. I lower Max, and she watches as he wraps around my forearm, her eyes wide. Then I spread her legs with my free hand and slowly lower Max between her parted thighs. "Tristan. No."

"You scared, Little Nun?" I ask her. She nods her head rapidly as I position Max where I want him. His head rests on her pelvic bone as the rest of his body is draped between her thighs. Then he slithers up over her soft belly and onto the mattress, sliding through her wetness.

Ash gasps at the feel of him moving over her. I can see she's afraid, trying to hold her breath, but she can't. Slowly, she begins to breathe but keeps her eyes clenched shut as the rest of Max's body slides across her naked breasts and then off the side of the bed.

I climb on the bed quickly, shoving my cock inside her as fast and as hard as I can without giving her any kind of notice.

"Tristan!" She screams my name just like I knew she would. She feels so good. So fucking good wrapped around me with nothing in between us. No condoms, no barriers, just us.

I spread her thighs further and get deeper inside her as she moans and pants for air. I pull out of her and flip her onto her stomach, lifting her ass up for me.

"What are you doing?"

"Different position, baby. You'll like it," I tell her before slapping my hand on her ass. She yelps just as I slide into her once more. Her pussy is clenching around me, and I don't know how long I'll be able to hold back when she's doing this.

I grip her hips in my hands roughly and begin to fuck her as hard as I was before. Her body bounces off me so perfectly I never want it to end, but I know this is new to her, and she won't hold out long.

"You going to cover my bare cock in your cum, Ash? You going to fucking make me as dirty as I make you?" I ask her. She doesn't answer, and I slap her ass once more. She cries out, and her pussy clenches again, holding me in a vise-like grip.

I take one hand and reach around, finding her pulsing clit ready for me. I play with it, circle it, and then I feel her tense. Her body drags me along for the fucking ride, sucking the cum right out of me. I groan as I fill her little pussy with me. Like this, there's nothing that could keep me from doing it again and again. Nothing at all between us. I'll never go back to condoms with her again. This is too raw. Too real.

I jerk inside her as she screams through her orgasm. When she calms down, her body goes limp, and I pull out of her, allowing her to fall onto the bed.

"Why did you do that?"

"What?"

"With the snake?"

"Why not? It was sexy as fuck watching him move over your body." She remains silent, and I get it. She doesn't know how she feels about it.

"What's it feel like having my cum sitting inside you?"

"What do you mean?"

"I didn't use a condom, Ash."

"Why not? I'm not on birth control!" She begins to freak out, but I just hold onto her, pulling her against me.

"It's fine."

"It's not! The last thing we need is a baby," she mouths off.

"Why? Don't want a crazy little bastard like me?" I snap at her, letting go of her and standing from the bed.

"You can't be serious," she asks, pulling the sheet over her chest and sitting up.

"Dead serious. You know, that's why my mom never had another kid. She was afraid."

"Tristan," she whimpers, but I want her softness. I don't fucking need it.

"Fuck it, Ash. Fuck it all!" I walk over and grab Max, placing him back in his tank before storming to the bathroom. I turn the water on and wash my face, trying to control the anger in me.

"I don't think there's anything wrong with you, Tristan." I huff a laugh and look over at her.

"After what I did to you? After what I plan on doing to you?"

"Which is?"

"Oh, now that's a surprise, Little Nun."

"I'm sorry your mom felt that way. It's just … I'm not ready for a baby," she tells me. I nod my head.

"I'll get you the morning-after pill."

"What is that?"

"It kills any chance you have of becoming pregnant," I inform her.

"Isn't that a sin?"

"Jesus, Ash. All we've been doing is sinning, and you're worried about killing my fucked up sperm?" I ask her.

She shrugs his shoulders as I dry my hands and walk over, pulling her into my arms. "Stop worrying so much. Just live."

"Okay. What are we doing now?" she asks, grinning up at me still.

"What do you want?"

"You."

"More of me?" She bites her lip, nods her head as I wrap my hand up in her hair, and tug her head back so she's looking up at me. "You want all of me, don't you? You want to see what it's like to fucking own me, but you know what? It's me who owns you."

"I want to own you too," she whispers.

"That'll never happen, Ash. I'm the man. I'm the one who will own every fucking part of you, and when my time comes, and I slip into hell gracefully, I'm taking every last drop of you with me."

Chapter 16
Ash

He's laughing. It's not something you hear from Tristan all the time, not a real laugh, anyway. And here he is, laughing. It's the perfect sound as we walk down the street with his arm around me.

Tristan has been showing me more of his life, what he does, where he goes, and who he's with. He even did something nice and stopped to get me ice cream.

For the most part, I think Tristan is misunderstood by many. Of course, he does erratic things, and sometimes they are beyond reason, but deep down inside of him, I think he has a good heart.

"So this is what you're doing now? Does Ben know about this?" I hear Tim's voice and stiffen in Tristan's arms.

"Who the fuck are you?" Tristan asks him.

"I could ask you the same," he responds, his eyes moving to me. I try to pull away from Tristan, but he doesn't allow it.

"You really cheating on Ben? Are you some kind of whore now?" As soon as the words leave his mouth, I know it means trouble.

Tristan pulls away from me and grabs his knife so quickly that I barely have a chance to respond.

"What did you just say to her?" he asks, pressing the knife to Tim's cheek.

"What are you going to do? Kill me?" Tim taunts, not knowing that he shouldn't.

"Call her something else, and I will. I will fucking gut you right here on the street and get away with it."

"I doubt that."

"Let's find out then, shall we?"

"Tristan, let's just go," I tell him, trying to pull his arm away from Tim. It's no use.

"I'm not done yet," he snarls at me. He presses the knife into Tim's cheek until he cries out in pain, and blood leaks down his face. I gasp as Tristan pulls back and wipes the flat edge of the blade across Tim's lips.

"I warned you. Don't make me warn you again."

"I'm calling the cops," he snivels.

"Good. Good for you," Tristan taunts him a little more before stepping back and shoving his knife back into the sheath. He turns to me, grabs my hand, and starts walking once more. I don't know what to say to him, so I say nothing. We keep walking, but neither of us says a word. I hear sirens, and my insides drop. Did he really call the police on him? Why wouldn't he?

"Stop overthinking it."

"How can I? You cut him, Tristan!"

"He's lucky that's all I did," he responds calmly.

"What else would you have done?"

"Just what I told him I would if he said another word."

"You're not a murderer." Now he laughs. And it's not a normal laugh. It's sick, dark, and depraved.

"Keep telling yourself that if it helps you sleep at night." I don't know what else to say to him.

We walk back to the warehouse, and he opens the door, ushering me inside, but I don't move. I stand in the doorway, unsure what to do.

"You scared of me, Little Nun?" he asks, turning to face me now.

"What was that back there?"

"That was me standing up for my girl. No one gets to call you a whore, Ash."

"But ... he was just being a jerk."

"A jerk who won't call you a whore anymore."

"But what if-" He cuts me off.

"What if, what if, what the fuck if!" He roars, raising two fingers to his head. He repeatedly taps himself in the head with the tips as he eyes me. "You're driving me insane! Do you want a man, Ash? Or you want a pussy because right now it's hard to fucking tell."

"Tristan, I just don't want anything to happen to you."

"Nothing's going to happen. Just calm the fuck down, Ash. You're too uptight. Little fuckers like him just like to show off, and they hate when someone like me knocks their ass back down a little."

"I don't know," I say softly. Tristan huffs and storms inside as I follow slowly behind him. He's across the room, lighting a cigarette before dropping into the chair.

"Why don't you strip for me."

"What?"

"Strip. For. Me."

"No."

"Why? It isn't like I haven't seen you naked, Ash."

"This isn't the time. We need to talk about this."

"We already did," he says, bringing his cigarette to his lips.

"We didn't. You can't go around cutting people, Tristan."

"Don't like it, there's the door, baby."

"Are you serious?"

"I'm dead serious." I know he's only saying that out of anger and that's fine. I get it. I'm pushing him more than most people would, but he can't keep doing this. He can't keep hurting others just because of something they said.

"I'm not leaving."

"Hmm."

"What's that mean?"

"Nothing. Strip for me."

"I'm not stripping for you!"

"Well, we're done fucking talking, so there isn't much else to do."

"Why can't you just talk to me?"

"Okay. Okay. Fuck. What do you want to talk about?"

"What goes on in that head of yours," I tell him. He laughs again and shakes his head.

"That's the last thing you want to hear about, Ash."

"I do want to hear about it."

"Why?"

"Because I care about you." Those words are like a brick to his chest. I can see the way the breath rushes out of him, and his eyes narrow on mine. He isn't sure what to say because he's not used to having anyone care about him. I know his mom loves him but I also believe she finds him a hindrance at times. I've heard her and my dad talking about him, not knowing how to handle him.

Tristan is one of those people who are hard to love, but I think deep down, he has a heart that needs all the love and caring it can get.

Chapter 17
Tristan

"So you slept with her?" Doc asks me as I shake my head.

"Not slept. Fucked."

"You fucked her?"

"That's exactly what I did to her. Multiple times, too, Doc."

"And how do you feel now?"

"Even more obsessed than I was before. I think if she asked me to jump off the goddamn bridge for her, I would do it."

"That isn't healthy, and I think you know that," he tells me.

"What does healthy mean?"

"It means that you have a clear path ahead of you, and that isn't just about obsession and what you want."

"You remember me telling you once before that I didn't give a shit what you thought? It's about time for you to hear it again, Doc. I'm me. I'm messed up. I'm fucked in the head. There's no curing me so why even try? You know what I like about Ash? She doesn't try to make me be something I'm not."

"She can't condone the things you do, does she?" he asks.

"Not everything, but she still doesn't try to talk her way into my head and fix something that can't be fixed."

"We can try other therapies, Tristan."

"Mock execution, electroshock therapy, role-playing. Nothing has worked, Doc. What makes you think something else would?"

"It's worth a try, isn't it?" I shake my head.

"No. I don't think it is. I think I'm too far gone and fucked up to be brought back to the real world."

"Is that what you feel? That you aren't in the real world?"

"I know I'm in the real world, asshole. You know it's just a saying." The buzzer rings, and I stand, saluting the asshole once more before heading out the door. It's October thirty-first. It's fucking Halloween night, and I have plans for Ash.

I hop on my bike and take off back to the warehouse, where she's waiting for me. Tomorrow, her little boyfriend comes back, but tonight, she's all mine.

I make it back and kill the engine, climbing off and heading inside. Ash sits on the couch, looking up and smiling when I walk in.

"How was your appointment?"

"Same as always," I reply. I walk over to the bed and grab the bag, tossing it to her.

"What's this?"

"Halloween costume," I tell her.

"I don't do Halloween, Tristan," she says.

"This year, you do. Put it on." She doesn't smile; she just opens the bag and pulls out the costume, holding it up in her hand.

"What is this?"

"A nun costume."

"Why?"

"Cause you're my dirty Little Nun, that's why."

"And this?"

"That's a collar."

"For what?"

"For you to wear."

"I don't think so."

"Oh, I fucking think so. I'm going to make you do so many dirty and disgusting things tonight, Little Nun. And you're going to look sexy as fuck with that around your neck," I tell her. Ash isn't sure what to do as I strip out of my clothes and put on my costume.

"Are you serious? A priest?"

"That's right, Little Unholy one. Tonight, you're going to pray at my altar."

Her cheeks turn pink as she stands and begins to change her clothes. This isn't classic nun attire. No, it's sluttier than she'd like, and I know it is.

I watch her get dressed, and then I walk over, grabbing the chain collar and looping it around her neck before pulling the end to tighten it. Her eyes widen before I lean down and drop a kiss to her lips.

"You look sexy as fuck in this. I'm going to love watching you sin for me," I tell her. Her cheeks heat even more, and I love that shade on her.

We finish getting ready, and then we head out, taking a taxi to the club. Ash has never been to a Halloween party, and I want her to have a good time.

We arrive and head inside meeting up with my friends when they arrive. The music is blasting, people are drinking, and the costumes are on fire. But nothing is hotter than Ash clinging to me the way she is. She's a little afraid, I can tell. This is all new to her. It isn't like the last time I brought her here. There are more people and less space.

I drag her out onto the dancefloor, and the two of us start dancing. For someone who doesn't get out, she can dance pretty well. My hands stay around her waist as she finally lets herself go and moves with the beat.

We get into a good rhythm, and I get lost in her. I'm always lost in her. I don't know how she does it, but she pulls me in like a fucking magnet. There's no way I can pull away from her. Not that I'd want to. I don't. I want her here, with me at all times. I want her in my arms. I want her in my bed. I want her in this fucked up head of mine because when I'm with her, everything else seems to calm.

"I think we need therapy," she laughs as I run my lips over her neck.

"No, we don't. You just need to feel my hand wrapped around your throat, your hair pulled, and to be told you're a good girl." Her lips part before I claim them with my own. I kiss her hard, hard enough that I'm sure her lips will bruise, and I don't give a shit.

It's like no one else exists right now. There's only me and her even in a room full of people. I couldn't care less about any of them. Just her. Always her.

"I want to go home," she whispers, and I pull back, looking confused.

"Home?"

"Your home. The warehouse."

"You're not having fun?" I ask her. She shakes her head, and I nod mine. I excuse us, and we leave quickly. I love Halloween but the ideas I have for my little nun tonight far outweigh my like of a holiday.

I make it home in record time before I get us inside and strip out of my clothes.

"Leave yours on," I tell Ash. She looks up at me, biting her lip, and I know what she wants. She wants to be fucked. I've created a little unholy monster with this girl.

I walk over to her, grabbing the knife off the table before backing her against the wall.

"Open your mouth," I tell her. She shakes her head, fear dancing in her eyes. Oh, I fucking love seeing her afraid. "Open," I demand this time. Her lips part, and I slide the handle into her mouth, and she closes her lips around it. I work it in and out of her mouth, letting her get used to feeling it there.

When I pull it free, I pull back and slam the blade into the wall next to her.

"Turn around and fuck the handle," I tell her.

"What? No."

"Oh, you're going to do it, Ash. And you're going to suck my cock while you do it."

"Tristan," she says softly.

"No. None of that shit. Just do what the fuck I tell you to do," I raise my voice at her. She nods her head and turns around, and I help her ease back onto the handle. It slips right into her wet pussy while she's bent over. I step back and watch her fuck the knife handle, and my cock grows harder. I've never seen anything so perfect in my life.

"Just like that," I tell her as I step closer, hitting her lips with my cock. Ash takes a shuddering breath before I shove it past her lips. Her tongue feels so fucking good touching me, but she gags a few times before she gets the hang of it.

"Breathe." She pulls air in through her nose as tears fill her pretty brown eyes. I don't stop just because she's crying. I keep going. I slide in and out of her mouth while she keeps fucking the knife handle. It's pure fucking perfection.

The more she sucks, the more I can't take it. Something about her being so fucking religious, and now she's here with my cock in her mouth? It's everything I could have dreamed of and more.

"Faster, baby," I tell her as I fuck her face so hard she can't breathe. I know she's close to coming, and that's exactly what I want. I want her cum all over my knife handle, and I want it now.

"Come on, Ash. Fucking cum on my knife." I force myself deeper into her, causing her body to push back onto the knife, and then she does it. She screams around my cock as she comes for me. Then I'm filling her mouth with my seed, and she's choking like a good girl on it.

"That's it. Good girl, Ash. Choke it all down," I tell her.

Chapter 18
Ash

Ben comes home today, and I have to find a way to tell him that we're over. My dad also comes home today, and I have to find a way to keep me and Tristan a secret, although he thinks we should tell them.

I don't. That's on me. That will be my punishment and I'm not sure I'm ready for that just yet.

Either way, things are going to change around here.

The doorbell rings, and I know it's Ben. I walk over, fixing my shirt, tugging it down to cover the top of the jeans I'm wearing. That should be a shock to him, to begin with. When I open the door and see him standing there, he eyes me up and down with a smile that quickly fades.

I step out onto the porch, and he hands me a bouquet of red roses.

"She prefers black now," Tristan smarts off behind me, but I ignore him and walk over to the porch swing to sit down.

"They are nice," I tell Ben. "Thank you."

"You're wearing jeans."

"They're nice, right?"

"I don't know what to say. I've never seen you wear jeans. Did your dad approve of this?" he asks.

"Not … not exactly."

"He doesn't know? Ash, this is asking for trouble. Go change," he says, nodding toward the door. I shake my head when Tristan walks out and sits on the chair across the porch from us.

"I'm comfortable in these."

"I think she looks sexy as fuck in those jeans," Tristan adds.

"No one really asked you," Ben retorts.

"Didn't need to."

"Can we have some privacy?" Ben asks. Tristan belts out a laugh that sends a chill down my spine.

"You want to be alone with her? Isn't that against the whole Godly thing?" He taunts him.

"Please," Ben says.

"No. I don't think so. As her older stepbrother, I take my duty of being her sibling very seriously, Ben. I wouldn't want any funny business going on," he tells him, a dark twinkle in his eyes. I almost laugh at his choice of words but cover it quickly with a cough. Tristan notices and smirks, but Ben doesn't.

"Fine. Stay then. So, how have the last few weeks been?"

"Have you spoken to Tim?"

"Tim? No. Why?"

"I was only wondering. I've seen him around, and before you left, I hadn't."

"I asked him to keep an eye on you," Ben explains.

"Why?" His eyes flick to Tristan and then back to me.

"Just to make sure everything was going okay."

"Okay. Enough of this shit. I can't sit here and be a party to this. It's fucking draining me," Tristan declares as he stands to his feet. He walks across the porch, rips me off the swing, and crashes his lips to mine. He kisses me so hard I can feel his teeth when they nip mine, drawing blood. I almost moan into his mouth, but I hold it back.

"What is this?" Ben roars as I pull back now. "You're with him?"

"Yeah, choir boy, she is. Now run along and say a prayer for all to be well tonight," Tristan tells him, rolling his eyes.

"This is insane, Ash! What are you thinking? What are you doing with someone like him? I knew I shouldn't have left you to this. To him! I should have stayed and protected you. It's not too late, Ash. We can fix this," he rambles as Tristan laughs. I slap at him, but he only laughs harder.

"She doesn't want you, pretty boy. Just go home. I mean, honestly, you're making yourself look like a fool right now. It's almost pathetic," Tristan adds.

"Does your father know? No. He would have punished you for this. You need to be punished for this," Ben sneers when Tristan moves. He wraps his hand around Ben's neck and slams him against the house.

"If I find out that either of you laid a hand on her, you'll be in an unmarked grave. You got me?"

"You think he's going to let you be with her? He won't. You're not one of us," Ben tells him.

"Unmarked, Ben. Your poor mommy won't know where to look for you, but I will, and I'll show up every fucking day just to piss on your grave. Hell, I might even fuck her over it," he tells him, my heart kicking up a notch.

"You won't get away with this," Ben warns before Tristan leans in and presses a kiss to his forehead.

"Get the fuck out of here before I make you my little bitch," he tells him. He releases Ben, and he turns, taking off down the steps.

"This isn't over," he calls out.

"Come back anytime, princess," Tristan tells him.

"What was that?"

"What was what?"

"You couldn't have waited for me to tell him?"

"Ash, it was becoming boring and you know I can't stand boring."

"You didn't even give me a chance," I tell him.

"Yeah, I did. You didn't take it. In fact, you took too long." I hear the car as it pulls into the driveway and I hurriedly glance down at my clothes before swallowing hard. I wasn't planning on staying in these clothes when they came home, but there's nothing I can do now.

Tristan steps closer to me, and I step back. His eyes move from mine to theirs and back again.

"Don't you dare," he growls low in his throat.

"I'll be punished."

"Like fuck you will be."

"Just let it happen, Tristan." I ignore his angry stare when my dad and Amy come up onto the porch. His smile fades first when he sees what I'm wearing.

"Get inside and get that off." No, hi, how are you? Are you okay? I knew this was coming, and I rushed inside, ready to take my punishment. I can vaguely hear Tristan and his mom talking on the porch when the screen door slams shut. I'm on my knees on the broomstick, praying to God he goes easy on me. A tear slides down my cheek when I hear the door close behind us.

The unmistakable sound of the whip flies through the air before snapping against my back.

"You've sinned. You've sinned against God!" My dad roars this time. Another snap, and the door flies open.

"Ash, stand the fuck up. Now." It's a demand from Tristan, but I don't know if I should do it. "Now!" He screams. I jolt and stand up, turning to face him as tears spill down my cheeks. Tristan stands there with a gun in his hand, scratching his head with the barrel as he looks between the two of us.

"You know, all I wanted for most of my life was for my mom to be happy." He glances at her where she stands in the doorway, her arms crossed over her chest. Then he turns back to my dad. "And out of all the son of a bitches in the world, she came across you."

"Put that down. It's not worth your own life," my dad tells him. Tristan laughs now.

"Oh, you thought this was about me? Oh no. This isn't about me. It's about you," he says, pulling the gun from his head and pointing it at my dad. I gasp, unsure what he might do because I know how much Tristan hates anyone touching me.

"What? What do you mean? What are you talking about?"

"When I fucked your little girl, I said to myself, no one is going to hurt her again. No one but me that is. And then you come back, swinging your little whip around and forcing her to kneel on the broomstick while I, on the other hand, force her to kneel for my cock," he tells him. I'm embarrassed. I don't know what to say or what to do. How to act. I'm just numb at this point.

"You what?" He yells as he steps toward Tristan but quickly rethinks it since he's still aiming the gun at him.

"Ash, go pack a bag," Tristan tells me. I quickly move through the room and fill a bag of my things before moving to stand by the door. "This was the last time, Ted. The last time you'll see her and certainly the last time you'll hurt her. If I ever, and I mean ever, catch you coming near her, well, you're a dead man."

"You can't take her!"

"She's twenty-one, and she's mine now! You hear me? Mine! She no longer has to live under your sick little rules. She no longer has to hide who she truly is. Try and stop me, and I swear to God this will be the best murder and suicide that you've ever seen." The anger in him is almost palpable. It's almost as if I could reach out and run my fingers through his darkness right now and there's a part of me that hurts for him. A part of me that screams to help him and do whatever I can to protect him and keep him safe.

Tristan walks backward, leaving my dad standing there stunned before turning to his mom.

"One hand on you, and you call me." She nods her head not bothering with arguing with him. He presses a kiss to her cheek and then motions for me to leave the room. I do so, quickly hurrying back to the front door, where Tristan follows.

We make it outside, and then we're heading to his bike as he shoves the gun into the back of his jeans. I grab the helmet and pull it on before climbing on behind him and wrapping my arms around his waist. This insane. I've never seen anything like what just happened here.

I hold on tightly while he pulls out of the driveway and takes off. I can tell by the direction we're going that we're headed back to the warehouse.

Chapter 19
Tristan

I pace the fucking floor with the unloaded gun in my hand, pressing it against my temple. I don't know what the hell I'm doing right now as Ash sits in the chair, curled into herself, watching me. She doesn't know it's not a loaded weapon anymore. It was at the house, and I regret not pulling the fucking trigger and taking her dad out.

I'm rambling to myself about what the fuck I'm going to do now because if he's willing to do that to Ash, why wouldn't he be doing it to my mom?

"I should have just done it. I should have shot him," I repeat for probably the fifth time in a row now.

"No, you shouldn't. I wouldn't have anyone then," Ash adds to my thoughts.

"You don't need me, Ash. What the fuck?" I ask her.

"You don't think so? Then what am I doing here?" she yells at me.

"You're here because I want you here!"

"And you don't care what I want? Right? You only care about what you want," she yells at me.

"It's not that you and know it."

"Then what is it?"

"Ash, how? How can you want someone like me? Huh?"

"How could I not is the better question."

"That doesn't make sense," I tell her.

"Tristan, don't you get it? I love you." Now I laugh. There's no fucking way she loves me. No one can love me. Not even I can love me.

"Don't laugh!" She yells as she climbs out of the chair and storms toward me. I don't think I've ever seen Ash this mad and I think I might like it.

"Why not?"

"I just told you I loved you. That's not something you laugh at, Tristan!"

"You can't love me, Ash. No one can."

"You're wrong because I do. And you can take it and warp it in any way your mind wants you to, but that doesn't change the facts," she tells me.

"What are the facts, Ash?"

"That I love you. You have given me something I never knew I wanted. You've set me free, Tristan. Don't you see that?"

"You know what I see? I see a little girl who lets her dad hit her because she still doesn't know who she is. You're standing in front of me now, lying to me."

"I'm not. Not about this." I toss the gun onto the couch and stomp toward her, gripping her face so hard it'll probably leave marks, but I don't care.

"You let him hurt you, Ash. That's something I said never to let happen again."

"It won't."

"It already has!"

"It won't again."

"You know, when I first saw you, I thought you were the one. I thought fuck, there's the girl I've always wanted and couldn't have. Then I saw what you let him do to you, and I thought, why? She's so much more than this, why?"

"What are you doing, Tristan?"

"You're never leaving me, Ash. Doesn't matter how fucked up I am. Doesn't matter if I hate you right now for letting him do that to you. Doesn't matter if my fucked up brain tells me to hurt you worse than him. You're never leaving!" I roar in her face. She flinches and tries to pull back, but I don't let her. I walk her over to the bed and pull my hand from her face, tossing her body onto the bed. Then I climb up quickly, grab the rope, and secure it around her wrist and the headboard.

"What are you doing?" she asks as tears stream down her cheeks.

"I just told you."

"You don't have to do this, Tristan. I don't want to leave."

"We'll see how you feel in a few days," I tell her, making sure the rope is tight enough that she can't get it undone.

"Tristan, please."

"Don't please me like I give a shit, Ash. Please means shit to me, and you know it."

"Don't do this. You don't have to."

"Oh, I have to." My mind is a buzzing mess right now. There's so much running wild that I don't know how to calm it and make it stop aside from the fucking medicine, and I don't plan on taking that.

I walk over and sit on the chair, resting my head in my hands and tugging at my hair. This has to stop, right? My mind has to slow down at some point. It can't keep going like this. Can it? I've never felt like this before. This is new, and I fucking hate it.

I sit, listening to her pleas as I tug at my hair until I feel like I'm going to rip it right out of my scalp.

"Shut up, Ash! Just shut up!" I scream at her. This isn't her fault, not really it isn't. It's mine. It's my fucked up head that's the problem right now. Maybe I need to call the Doc? No, fuck him. He'll just want to shock me or some shit again, and that shit didn't work last time.

I close my eyes now that Ash has shut up. I'm about to break down. I'm searching for a way out of my head.

I'm falling apart, and I can't stop it. What the hell can I do?

"I love you," I hear Ash say once more. I cringe at her words. She loves me. Maybe she does, but I can't see how. I'm not loveable. I've done things to her, things that would send her straight to hell, and that's where I want her, in my hell.

I look up at her, staring at me. I stand from the chair and walk over, grabbing her shoes and pulling them off. Then I move to her jeans next to pull them off with her panties.

"Spread your legs," I order her softly. She does as I say, and that makes me smile. She knows how to listen like a good girl, doesn't she?

I scoot between her legs and slap my hand on her pussy.

"Tristan!"

"Does it hurt?"

"A little." Another slap and I watch her body tense.

"Good. I want to hurt you, Ash."

"Why?"

"To make you feel good. To make me feel better."

"Do what you need to do, Tristan," she tells me. I hop off the bed and dig through the drawer, finding the candles and a lighter. I light them, set them on the table, and then turn back to Ash. I rip open the front of her shirt and then grab my knife, cutting her bra off. She watches me, her breathing becoming faster by the second.

When she's exposed to me, I lean down and bite her nipple hard enough to draw blood. Ash whimpers, and when I look up, I see the tears in her eyes she's trying not to let fall.

Then I reach for the candle and bring it over her chest. Tipping it sideways, I let the hot wax fall onto her flesh and watch her lips part.

"Tristan," she cries my name, and fuck, it sounds so right.

"It's okay, Ash." I keep going, pouring hot wax over parts of her body and watching it set on her skin. But when it's not enough, I set it back on the table and spread her legs, pushing my jeans and boxers down and grabbing my cock.

"You love me, Ash?" I ask her before slapping her pussy with my cock. She gasps, and I do it again and again. "Tell me."

"Yes!" she squeals as I keep slapping her. Then I shove into her and fuck her hard. I need this. I need her. What the hell is wrong with me?

Chapter 20
Ash

Things with Tristan have been strange the last couple of weeks. He's been distant and not speaking much. In fact, he's barely touched me, and it makes me wonder if he's really over me now.

He untied me from the bed the same night and held me for almost a full day. It was crazy, but I let him have his time. He wouldn't accept the fact I love him, and I know that's a tough one for him, so I'm just giving him time.

He's been lost in his work, sculpting all day and most of the night, which I guess is what he does when he's stressed. I just feel bad I'm the reason he's so stressed.

I walk toward the door, grabbing my jacket as I go, ready to head out and grab us something to eat.

"Where the hell are you going?" His voice sends a chill down my spine. I both love and hate when he talks to me like that.

"To get food."

"We can order it."

"We haven't left the warehouse in weeks, Tristan. I'm bored." He stops what he's doing and looks at me intently before nodding.

"I'll take you out," he offers. A genuine smile crosses my face as I watch him go clean up and then come back. He's ready, opening the door for me and ushering me outside.

"Walking?" I ask, hopeful. It's been so long since we've walked and done anything that I think we just need that break. He nods, and we start walking when some asshole whistles at me. Tristan turns, pulling his knife once more and grabbing the guy's face. He pries his mouth open and grabs his tongue, resting the blade on it.

"You whistle at my girl one more time, and I'll cut your tongue out," he growls at him. I gasp, watching the scene unfold, but it doesn't really surprise me anymore. This is Tristan, although I haven't seen this side of him in a while.

He presses the knife against the man's tongue, and I can see the blood blooming before Tristan pulls the knife away. The guy doesn't say anything; he just takes off running in the opposite direction.

"Are you okay?" I ask him.

"Why wouldn't I be?"

"You haven't been for weeks," I remind him.

"I'm great, baby. Just give me some time, okay?" I nod my head and we keep walking until we reach the diner. He opens the door and ushers me inside and over to a table. We sit down and order as I stare at him.

"What?"

"Nothing."

"You're starting at me," he says.

"I know."

"Then stop."

"I don't want to." Now, he looks up at me and grins.

"Why?"

"You're beautiful."

"You're beautiful," he says, causing my heart to leap in my chest. This is the Tristan I've missed. The one I want to, although I'll take any version of him I can get.

"I've missed this," I tell him. He nods his head knowing what's been happening the last few weeks. It hasn't been easy on either of us.

"I know. I'm working on it," he says as I nod my head now.

"Do you want to do something tonight?" I ask him.

"Like what?"

"I don't know. Anything."

"There's an art show downtown if you want to go to that. I know how much you love art," he says.

"I'd like that."

"We need to talk too."

"About what?"

"You haven't been going to school." I look down at the table because I can't look at him. Strangely, I haven't felt like going. I want to spend my time with Tristan, which I know is insane, especially all the time.

"I haven't felt much like going."

"Because of me."

"Not just that."

"What then?" he asks, and I shrug. It is that. I don't want to walk away from him. I don't know why there's this ache in my chest when he isn't near, but I want to keep it at bay.

"I don't know, honestly. I love art. It would make sense I want to go, right? But I don't. Anyway, I've been doing some work online."

"Do you want to sculpt with me?" he blurts, taking me by surprise.

"Really?"

"Why not? You don't seem to want to leave my side, so you might as well get paid for your time stalking me," he teases with a gorgeous grin on his face.

"Stalking you? Is that what we're calling it?"

"Yeah. I see the way you look at me, Ash."

"How do I look at you?" I ask him, wanting to know what he sees.

"With love."

"So you get it now?"

"I get it now," he tells me, and my heart nearly bursts. I lean over the table and press my lips to his savoring the taste of him on my tongue.

"Climbing tables now, are we?"

"I'd climb through anything for you," I inform him. He grins and shakes his head.

"Don't do that for me, Ash. Do it for you." I don't know what that means, and I don't really care. I sit back down, and we finish our meal before heading out. We're walking down a back alley when I hear a noise behind us.

Tristan hears it, too, pulling me into his side.

"Don't move," I hear Ben's voice. Instantly, I freeze. We both turn to see Ben standing there with a gun aimed at me.

"What is this choir boy? Doesn't this go against your religion?" Tristan chuckles.

"You think this is all fun and games, right? That I won't kill you because I will. You stole something from me, and it's time I take it back."

"Like fuck you will. I'll see you in hell before I let you touch her," Tristan growls, and it sends a chill down my spine.

Ben steps closer, and that's when I hear it. Someone else is moving around behind us. The shot is fired before anyone can think or move. Tristan roars and rushes at Ben, but another shot is fired, and he goes down.

"Tristan!" I scream as I'm grabbed from behind. I try to fight whoever is behind me, but it does no good. Something is placed over my face, and I find myself losing all sense of belonging.

"Tristan," I manage to mumble once more before everything goes black.

Chapter 21
Tristan

I groan as I move my arms a little, only to find that I'm tied down. Prying my eyes open, I look to see what the hell is going on when I see where I am.

"Not the fucking hospital again," I grumble. One of the places I hate the most is the damn hospital.

"You're awake. We can take these off then," I hear the Doc say next to me. I turn my head to look at him and smirk.

"Did you think I did this to myself, too?" I ask him with a grin.

"No. You were combative when they brought you in."

"With good reason," I tell him, thinking about Ash.

"Which is?"

"I was shot, Doc. Twice, I might add. I'm like a goddamn cat with nine lives, and I've already used half of them," I admit to him. He chuckles, knowing I'm not wrong about that.

"What happened?"

"I don't know. Dude came out of nowhere, demanded my wallet, and I told him to fuck himself. He shot."

"That's terrible, Tristan. I can't believe it." He shouldn't believe it. I'm a liar. He should already know that. I also won't give him or the cops the truth because that kill is mine. Not theirs.

I know that Ben and her dad have her. I just need to find out where and end the miserable bastards.

"You sure it wasn't something more?" he asks. He must be watching me intently, even though I'm lost in my head.

"What do you think happened?" I challenge him. He doesn't know, and he will never know because I won't be the one telling him.

"I don't know. I was only asking. The police wanted to speak with you." I shrug.

"Fine. Send them in." He stands and leaves, sending them in, and I tell them the same story I told the Doc. They aren't getting shit out of me. This is something I'm going to handle on my own.

When they finally leave, I lay my head back to rest when the door opens once more. I wish it were her. I wish it were Ash, but I know that it isn't.

When I see who it is, I'm actually a little shocked.

"Mom?"

"How are you feeling?"

"Tired and sore. What are you doing here?"

"He's hurting her, Tristan. I … I can't do that. I can't watch that."

"What do you want to do?"

"I want him out. I want him in jail. I thought about calling the police," she whispers, breaking down in tears. I reach for her hand and pull her closer to me.

"No cops, mom. I'm going to take care of this," I tell her.

"How?"

"How do you think? Where are they?"

"At the house. They have her in the basement, tied up, Tristan. They are forcing her to repent for her sins. They're making her do things…it's too much. I can't see that happening to her," she cries harder.

"I'm going to handle it, Mom. I just need a few days to get out of here."

"I can … I can try to distract him."

"Yeah. Do that. Let me get out of here, and I'll take care of it. I promise."

"Okay. I'll do what I can," she says as I nod my head. She sits down and stays a bit with me while I send off a text to Andy and Rod that I'm going to need help soon. They both agree and say they're coming to see me soon anyway, and we can discuss it then.

I send my mom home after she nearly falls asleep in the chair, but not before reminding her not to call the cops.

She agrees even though she doesn't want me in trouble. It doesn't matter now. I know she's back at the house. I plan on fucking their world up when I get out of here.

I close my eyes and picture her face. Fucking Ash. What did I do to deserve that girl? Nothing. I didn't do a damn thing to make her want me, but she does. She wants me, of all fucking people. The one who's the most fucked up.

"You asleep?" I open my eyes when the Doc comes back in.

"I didn't know you made house calls," I fuck with him a little.

"When I need to. Anything you feel like talking about?" Dr. Hassan has always tried to help me in any way he could. He's unconventional and basically a bastard, but he does try.

"She said she loved me."

"Did you say it back?"

"No."

"Why not? Do you not love her?"

"I don't know what the fuck that means. I mean, I love my mom, right?"

"You say you do, but I tend to agree with you that you don't know what it means."

"So tell me."

"It's different for everyone. Some say it's like losing your mind when they aren't near you. Some say it's the strongest thing they've ever felt when they are with you. It's very different for each person," he tells me.

"I hate it when she isn't with me."

"That doesn't mean love. That just means you want what you want."

"Did you come back to fuck with my head a little more?" I snap at him. He shakes his head.

"No. I wanted to see if you really needed to talk."

"I want her, Doc. With me every second of every day. I don't like it when she isn't there. It feels like a part of me is empty," I admit to him.

"Then I'd say you love her, Tristan. In your own way, of course."

"But?"

"But you're complicated. Your mind is different than most people's."

"And that's a bad thing?"

"In some cases, yes. In others, no."

"And with her? You think it's bad, right?"

"I don't know what to think. I've never seen the two of you interact before. Maybe one day, when you're feeling better, you can bring her to a session," he suggests. I snort a laugh. Fat fucking chance of that happening. Ash doesn't need to know just how fucked up I truly am by meeting with him.

"Doubt that," I tell him.

"I figured that much. But it's always an option if you change your mind. Get some rest. I heard you were here for two days," he tells me. I nod my head and watch him stand and leave. I don't want him here any longer than he needs to be because I need to make plans with Andy and Rod to get this shit on the road.

As soon as he's out of the room, I call the guys again and start talking. I tell them that I want her out of that house, and I want the two of them tied up at the warehouse until I get out of here.

They agree to handle it, and I close my eyes, trying to get some sleep, but it doesn't happen. I'm too lost. Too fucked in the head to sleep, so I don't. I stay awake and let the insomnia fuck me over a little more.

Chapter 22
Ash

Tears continue to roll down my cheeks as the whip slices my back. It isn't just my dad this time; it's Ben, too. He keeps yelling bible verses at me and telling me to repent for my sins. I want Tristan, and to be honest, that's the only thing that's kept me going. The idea of him.

His mom has told me he's okay, but they won't release him for a few days, and he isn't well enough to check himself out. Another crack, and I scream this time.

"That's about enough of that shit," I hear his voice, and it washes over me like warm water. Ben turns at the same time as I do to see Tristan and his friends standing there. He looks good but tired and I can understand that. He was shot. Twice.

"Tristan," I cry as he makes his way closer, using a cane to walk. My heart hurts for him because I know it was my fault he was shot.

"Don't move!" Ben roars as he holds the whip in his hand. Tristan laughs.

"A whip? You think I don't like being whipped every once in a while?" he asks him, and my eyes widen. I've never thought of that. Tristan is into all kinds of things, why not that, too?

"I'll end you," Ben tells him as the others laugh.

"You and who? We already got your little friend up there," Andy tells him, pointing upstairs. Andy and Rod converge on Ben while Tristan comes to me. He leans down and helps me up the best he can, wincing the whole time.

"I thought you couldn't leave?"

"Did you really think I'd leave you to this another day?" he asks as he wraps me in his arms and kisses my cheek. "Your hell is with me. Not here."

I want to smile, but I can't. I hurt too badly to do that. Tristan finds me a shirt and helps me pull it on while the guys round up Ben and my dad. Tristan helps me up the stairs as best he can when he sees his mom.

"I'm sorry it has to be this way," he tells her.

"No. Don't be sorry, Tristan. You tell me what to do, and I'll do it. She deserves better than this," she says, nodding toward Ted, where he has a gag in his mouth.

"I'll let you know." She nods her head and looks over at me giving me a sad smile as if she's sorry she couldn't have stopped this. My dad was too strong. There was no way she could have stood up against him.

I give her a sad smile in return as Tristan leads me out of the house and toward a van out front. We both climb in while the others load them into the back after tying them up, then they, too, climb in, and we take off.

"Are you okay?" I ask him. He shakes his head, and I understand what he means. Not physically but mentally. He's falling apart, and I get that.

We ride until we make it to the warehouse, and I shake my head.

"We live here," I remind him.

"Oh, Little Nun. We're still going to live here with the ghosts of these bastards haunting us at night," he explains before climbing out. I don't know how I feel about all of this. He's going to kill them, that much I am sure of, and that's my dad and my ex.

I follow Tristan inside and watch as the guys drag the others inside and tie them to chairs. The same chairs we've sat in to have dinner are now holding the two men I hate the most in the world.

"Why here?" I ask. Tristan comes toward me, wrapping his hand around my throat and tugging me toward him.

"This is it, Little Nun. This is the end of the line here. I thought about killing them somewhere else, but what better reminder of what I've done than doing it in my own space?" he asks me.

"Tristan."

"You don't have to see, baby. I won't make you watch."

"But I'll know!"

"And does that change how you feel about me? Hmm? Do you not love me anymore after what I plan to do because I fucking love you, Ash."

"You what?"

"You heard me, baby. I love you. I didn't think I could. I didn't think that's what this was but it is because I'd rather live my life clawing at the gates of hell to get back to you than to be without you." My heart bursts inside of me at his words. He loves me. I wasn't sure if Tristan could love, but he loves me. I nod my head as tears spring to my eyes, and I press my lips to his.

"You taste so good," he says against my mouth before kissing me harder. When he pulls away, I walk over and sit on the couch so I'm out of the way. Tristan glances over and smirks at me before pulling his knife from the sheath and pointing it at Ben.

"You were the last person I thought would do this to her, but here we are," he states, using his other hand to hold the cane as he walks around him.

"You don't know a thing! She needed this," he roars as Tristan laughs.

"Needed it? The only thing she needs is me," he tells him.

"You are the devil incarnate!"

"And she loves every deep, dark thing I do to her. I could draw this out, but frankly, I'd rather have her riding my cock than dealing with this shit," he tells them as my cheeks heat.

"Both of you are going to rot in hell!" my dad yells this time.

"Then I'll meet you there, Ted," Tristan says before slitting Ben's throat and moving to my dad next. I can't look, so I don't. I look down at my hands, but I can hear him gagging. My insides lurch, and I start moving toward the bathroom in a hurry. Once I'm in there, I throw up. I lose everything I have in me which isn't much.

I hug the toilet when I hear Tristan walk in.

"Weak stomach?" he asks playfully.

"Are they .... is he ...."

"They're dead. Both of them. The guys will get it cleaned up before you have to go back out there."

"And their bodies?"

"Don't worry about it. You don't need to know," he tells me before doing his best to kneel next to me. I see him wince, and I know he's still in pain, but he doesn't let on at all. Instead, he slides to the floor and grabs me, pulling me into his arms.

"You're hurt," I whisper.

"No more than you are."

"You were shot twice," I remind him.

"You were beaten. I'm sorry, Ash. I should have been there. I should have been there to handle that shit."

"It's not your fault."

"It is, though, and I'm so fucking sorry."

"Stop saying that. You have nothing to be sorry for."

"You're right. And just because you're being a brat, I'm going to spank your pussy and force you to come more times than you can actually count."

"You think you can with a bad shoulder and leg?"

"I'm the devil incarnate, didn't you hear? I can do anything I want."

"What about love me? Can you do that?"

"Isn't that what I'm already doing?"

"Yeah, you are. I love you, Tristan."

"Love you too, Little Nun."

Chapter 23
Tristan

Sometimes, I sit and wonder how it would feel to let go. Sometimes, I find myself back at the gates of hell where I belong. Others, I find myself hiding in plain sight.

Most days, I know who the fuck I am but others? I don't know shit. I'm struggling again. Not because I killed those fuckers, but because taking on Ash has been hitting me hard.

She's changing, and it isn't that I don't like it; I do, but she doesn't know who she is anymore. Doesn't know where she belongs, and she's doing everything she can to fit in. And a part of me hates that shit.

"You don't have to fucking fit in, Ash! How many times do I have to say it?"

"Apparently, more than one."

"Why do you want to fit in so badly? Huh? I don't fucking fit in, and I could care less," I remind her.

"I want to have friends, Tristan. I want to go out and be a damn twenty-two-year-old girl!" Yeah, she celebrated her birthday by riding my cock with a candle up her ass, and she enjoyed every fucking minute of it.

"Then go!"

"I will!" She roars before grabbing her jacket and storming out the door. I chuckle and walk over, waiting for her to come back, which she does seconds later.

"You know what? I hate you." Now I laugh harder.

"No, you don't. You hate yourself."

"Why would I hate myself, Tristan?"

"Because you don't know who you are unless you're getting your ass whipped," I remind her. She tries to step back, but I grab the chain around her neck and pull it, choking her a little. She reaches up to grab it, and I shake my head, her hands slowly lowering back to her sides.

"Get on your knees," I demand. At first, she doesn't do it, but when I snap the chain in my hand a little harder, she drops in front of me. "Pull my cock out," I tell her. She licks her lips and reaches up, unzipping my jeans and pulling my cock free. Then she leans in, and I step back.

"Did I tell you to lick it?"

"Seriously, Tristan?"

"Fine. Go ahead, baby. Show me what a dirty little nun you really are." She wraps her lips around my cock and slowly begins to suck. She's done it a few times before this, but not often. I don't make her do it because it's more fun when I eat her pussy and make her crazy. Like this, she knows she has some kind of control, and I don't give her that all the time.

She keeps sucking as I let my head drop back, enjoying what she's doing to me. Her tongue flattens along the vein, and I nearly come down the back of her throat.

"Come on, Ash. I want to come today," I tell her. She keeps going until I do. Shooting my load down the back of her throat. She's gagging, and I love every second of it. I want to cut off her air supply. I want to make her uncomfortable, and I do.

When I'm done and she can't breathe, I pull out of her mouth and slap her cheek with my cock.

"The next time you want to be a brat, just drop to your knees, Ash."

"I'm not being a brat." She stands in front of me, cum leaking down her chin, and I groan from the sight. I lean in and lick it off her before kissing her and shoving it all in her mouth. Ash groans and pulls me closer to her.

"I want you, Tristan.

"You have me, baby."

"No. I want all of you."

"What do you mean?"

"I want to marry you. I want everything with you, Tristan."

"It's a good day for an unholy black wedding."

"Are you serious? Can we get married?"

"Ash. Come on. I'm not the marrying type."

"But you're also not going to let me go either?"

"Fuck no. Is that what you want? After everything I've done for you?" I yell a little louder than I need to. She's making me mad, and not in a good way.

"No, that's not what I want, asshole. I just told you I wanted to marry you!"

"I really do like your new vocabulary, Ash."

"Shut up."

"I mean it. It's sexy as hell hearing you say those words," I tell her, calming both of us. A smile tugs across her face before she speaks.

"I didn't know it could be so empowering."

"Just say what you feel, right?" She nods her head, and that's all I can take. I pull her against me, holding her there for as long as I feel like. I press my lips to the top of her head and sigh, just breathing her in.

"Are you okay?" she whispers, and I know what she's talking about. She thinks I'm losing my mind after everything that happened, but she could be more wrong. I'm okay. I feel okay, and killing them didn't bother me the way she thought it would. Hell, it doesn't feel like I did anything out of the normal.

"I have a bad feeling," I tell her, not wanting to admit to it.

"About what?"

"Everything that happened. I'm not sure Andy and Rod know how to get rid of bodies the way they should."

"And you're just now thinking about this?" She freaks out. I hold onto her tighter, not letting her go.

"Yeah, I am. Maybe I'm wrong. I could be wrong, but I don't think they've ever hidden bodies before."

"I don't want to talk about this," she says, burying her face in my shirt.

"It's fine. Fuck, even if they find them, what?"

"You could go to prison, Tristan." Now I laugh.

"Like I'd ever let that happen. I'd die before I went to prison," I tell her.

"Don't say things like that."

"It's the truth, Ash."

"You'd rather be dead than get to see me?"

"If I'm locked up, I'm not seeing you anyway. Just drop it, okay? I'm sure it's fine. You ready to go?" I ask her. I promised her a ride on the bike, and I plan on giving her that. She nods her head, and we break apart before heading outside. I grab the helmet and pass it to her, eyeing her while she puts it on. I can't get enough of her wearing jeans. They hug her perfect ass, and that's all I can ever look at it. It makes her laugh, and that's the best sound in the world.

I climb on, and she climbs on behind me, wrapping her arms as tightly as she can around my waist and holding on while I take off.

We ride around for a little while when I hear sirens behind me. I'm so close to the bridge that I don't pull over until I'm on it. Ash is tense, her arms tight around me until the cops pull up and surround us.

"Off the bike," comes a man's voice. I knew it. One of them either turned on me, or they didn't hide the bodies well enough. Fuck!

Ash climbs off only after I tell her to. Then I climb off, pulling her helmet from her head.

"Hands in the air!" Comes the next command. I smirk and look down at Ash.

"You know I love you."

"Whatever you're about to do, don't. We don't know that's what this is about."

"Yeah, we do. Tell me you love me," I tell her.

"Don't do this," she begs softly.

"Tell me," I demand this time.

"I love you, Tristan." I lean down and capture her lips with mine, kissing her so hard she'll never be able to forget me. When I pull back, I shove her away from me toward the cops.

"She had nothing to do with it! Don't hurt her!"

"Hands up! Or I'll shoot!" Now I laugh. Shoot? Hell, I've been shot. That isn't going to happen again either, that shit hurt.

"Tristan."

"Put your hands up and walk over there, Ash." She starts to move, and so do I. I climb the rail just as she turns to face me. I blow her a kiss, and then shots are fired just as I jump.

The freefall is something I've never felt in my life. The free feeling, the rushing through the air. I close my eyes as everything blows past me, and then I straighten out and hit the water.

Chapter 24
Ash

There was no funeral. There was no body. The cops commented no one could have survived that fall. Maybe they're right. Maybe he's resting now at the bottom of the fucking water, I don't know.

I've been in the basement at Amy's because I couldn't stand to be alone at the warehouse. She's having a hard time with letting him go, too, and I can't say that I blame her. I wasn't ready to say goodbye. I wasn't ready to let him go either, but he did what he did, and that really wasn't a shock to me.

I look up at the painting on the wall and smile a little. It's perfect. Just like him. A fallen angel who never got the chance to be more. And Tristan could have been a lot more.

"Hey." Amy's voice filters through my thoughts.

"Hi."

"We need to talk," she says as she comes to sit next to me, placing her hand on my knee. "The warehouse. Did you want to keep it for yourself?" she asks me.

"No."

"I didn't figure so. I don't really want to sell it either," she adds.

"I'll burn it down."

"What?" she asks, sounding confused. I look over at her and give her a sad smile.

"I'll burn it down. You can collect the insurance money, and no one can ever live in there again," I reply softly.

"Is that what you want?"

"Yeah. I don't want anyone else in his space."

"Your space. You shared that space with him, and I've never seen him as happy as he was then," she adds.

"I was happy too," I tell her as a tear slides down my cheek. I reach up and quickly wipe it away.

"He loved you, Ash."

"I loved him. Every single broken piece of him." She nods and wraps her arm around my shoulder, pulling me into her side.

"I can't believe he's actually gone. That man tempted death so many times it was unreal." She lets out a little laugh, but it isn't a happy one.

"You're right. He did. I'm going to go and handle the warehouse. Did you want anything out of it?" I ask her. She shakes her head as I stand and grab one of Tristan's bags, stuffing a lighter and matches just to be safe inside. I grab one of his hoodies and slip it over my head, smiling at Amy before I head for the steps.

When I get outside and climb in my car, I lose it. I scream, I cry, I bash on the steering wheel. The selfish bastard. He didn't have to do that. He didn't have to leave us the way he did. Leave me. How the hell could he have left me after everything that happened between us? Did he think I'd just recover from that?

Anger surges in my veins as I pull out and head to the warehouse. I'm mad now. More than mad.

It doesn't take me long to reach the warehouse, climb out, and head inside. I glance around at everything. His work, his unfinished sculptures. The knife that's stuck in the wall that he made me fuck. That one causes a smile to cross my face.

I had already donated his snakes to a children's zoo, so I didn't have to kill them or look at them.

I pull out the matches and light one, watching it flicker to life before tossing it at the wall. The dark curtains he had hanging immediately catch fire and I smile.

"You left me to this. You left me to do your fucking dirty work. You left me to clean up your fucking mess!" I scream as the fire climbs the walls.

"What did you think about when you jumped, Tristan? It sure as hell wasn't about me!"

I flick another match to life and toss it across the room, watching all his shit burn.

When the smoke becomes too much for me to deal with and the coughing sets in, I head out of the warehouse and jump in my car. I drive down the block, far enough away no one will notice me, and then I park the car to watch it all go up in flames.

"You would have wanted it like this, right? Nothing left of the old life you lived? You never told me. You never told me what you wanted on the off chance you died. Then you went and did it yourself, you bastard."

Now I laugh a little. Only Tristan could get me laughing like this about saying curse words.

How can you not call him what he was, though? Bastard. That's what he was for leaving me, but deep down, he was so much more than that.

Tristan was a force to be reckoned with. He lived in a world all his own, and even right now, as his warehouse burns and tears spill down my cheeks, he's no longer facing his demons; he's living with them, thriving with them.

If we're being honest, he's probably running the show wherever he is.

THE END

Hope you enjoyed that fucking rollercoaster ride.

Are you shitting me? You're mad that he's dead? Where the fuck else would he be? He JUMPED off the fucking bridge, people!

Whatever. You don't like that ending? Read the Epilogue then. Needy bitches …

Epilogue

Ash

Five months. Five of the loneliest months I've ever experienced.

Amy got a new job at some ministry, which I was happy about for her. Me? I was never going back to that life. Not that I don't believe, I do. I just can't go back to what I used to be.

Tristan changed me in ways I never knew was possible, and there's no way I can take that part of myself away again.

"This is for you," Amy says, passing me an envelope. I look at it strangely and then at her, but she just shrugs.

"Where'd it come from?"

"I don't know, honestly. It was slid under the door," she replies. What the hell? Whoever is playing games had better stop. I'm not in the mood and I may just go off the rails today.

I rip open the envelope and find a one-way ticket to Mexico tucked inside and I immediately laugh.

"Yeah, I'm dumb enough to get on a one-way flight to Mexico alone?" I laugh as I pass the ticket to Amy. She looks it over and shrugs, passing it back.

"Who would have done that?"

"Some weirdo, obviously."

"Are you going?"

"You want me to get killed? Trafficked by the cartel?" I ask her, and she laughs.

"What if it's an old friend?"

"There's no name!"

"You should live a little. Besides, if it's sketchy when you get there, come back. I'll even buy the ticket back here." With that, she stands and walks off, making me think she knows exactly what the fuck this is and where it came from. Is she trying to tell me something? That I need to move out, maybe? Have I overstayed my welcome with her?

We've never had an issue before, but I don't know. I glance down at the ticket and see the flight is for tonight. She's not giving me much time to even think about it. This has to be from her. Maybe she needs a break.

I sigh. Maybe I have overstayed. Maybe she does need the space. Thinking it's for the best, I walk over and grab my suitcase and pack it. She wants me gone? Fine. I'll go. But I'm coming back. I'm not just going to stay down there. She'd be insane if she thought that.

I grab my things and drag them upstairs to where she sits in the living room, a smile on her face.

"You're going?"

"Only if you tell me this ticket is from you," I tell her.

"Partially from me. Think of it as a gift to you. You can come back anytime," she says. I smile at her before thanking her and pulling her into a hug.

The next thing I know, I'm on a freaking plane heading to Mexico. There better be cabana boys where she sent me who will run and grab my drinks when I want them. The thought of Tristan sitting next to me while they did all the work makes me laugh. Mainly because I know he's going to have something smart to say about them.

The plane lands, and I walk off the plane and head to baggage claim to find my stuff. When I grab it off the carousel, the scent of someone's cologne wafts past me. I spin around and look, swearing that's the same kind Tristan used to wear, but I don't see anyone.

Ignoring it, I walk toward the door when it happens again. I spin around once more, but I don't see anyone out of the ordinary. I must be losing it. I have to be.

I keep walking until I reach the door, and as soon as I step outside, someone says, "Know where you're headed?" That voice sends a chill down my spine.

I turn and look and there he is standing with a cane. How is this possible? I watched him jump. There's no way he could have made it.

"Tristan," I whisper his name as if he's not here standing in front of me. "How …"

"Come here, Ash," he says, holding his arm out for me while keeping the other on the cane. I step toward him, and then he's there, pulling me into his arms. He holds me, keeping me pressed close to his body, and I savor every second of it. His lips press into my neck, and I begin to cry.

"How are you here?" I whisper against him, not wanting to let him go. I never want to let him go again.

"Long story. Short version: I broke my leg on the landing and had to heal, but I knew the cops would be after me, so I took what I had and left."

"You made it here?"

"Yeah. Had some help, but I made it. And now you're here," he tells me. I pull back and shove at him, pissed and angry.

"You let us think you were dead! I could kill you, Tristan!" I yell at him.

"Shh. Don't yell out my name like that, Little Nun. You want me to be dead for real?" I cover my mouth quickly as he begins to laugh. The asshole. I shove him once more before he uses his free arm to pull me back into him. His kiss is like fire and everything I've missed about him.

"Does your mom know?"

"She does now. Well, at least a few weeks now. I couldn't risk anyone finding out. She'll be coming down soon, too."

"Are you serious?"

"Yeah, I am. This is it, Ash. This is all I've ever wanted. You, my family. You're everything to me, Ash."

"I love you, Tristan."

"I love you too. Now, let's go, so you can drop to your fucking knees and pray at my altar, Little Nun."

"You're still on that Little Nun thing, huh?" I ask him playfully.

"The day Lucifer drags my ass to hell and slams the gates closed is the day I'll stop with it. You've always been my little slutty nun, haven't you?"

"Slutty?" Now he laughs.

"You know how much I've missed you?" he asks now.

"Not as much as I've missed you."

"Oh, Ash. You've learned nothing about me, have you?"

"What do you mean?"

"I mean, I did it all for you. I crawled out of hell on my hands and knees, digging through the dirt just to get back here to you. Do you know the doctor said I should be dead after that jump?"

"What doctors?"

"The one's here. You think I would have gotten treated back home? Shit, they would have locked my ass up, Ash. I had the guys get me the fuck out of there and down here as quickly as possible."

"Are you insane?" I ask him. Now, he laughs hysterically.

"You know I am, baby. You fucking love me anyway."

Printed in Great Britain
by Amazon